**Ida Pollock** was born near London i
10 she knew that she wanted to be a
of her stories were published in maj
a variety of interesting figures, am
then Book Editor at George Newnes, but ambition and other factors
were at the time driving her to the edge of a breakdown. Travelling
alone to Morocco, she glimpsed the desert and the Atlas mountains
before returning home, cured, to embark upon a secretarial course.

Jobs in Harley Street and Wimpole Street were followed by a stint at
the Law Society, and as World War II broke out she stayed on, working
through the Blitz, until a chance encounter with Hugh Pollock turned
her life round again. Back in the Army, Hugh had been appointed
Commandant of a school for Home Guard officers, and feeling Ida
should be out of London he offered her a post as civilian secretary. She
accepted, and as the months went by their relationship intensified. In
May 1942, Hugh was sent overseas and Ida came close to being killed
by a bombing raid, but following Hugh's divorce from Enid Blyton he
and Ida were married in October 1943. Soon they had a daughter and as
the war ended her life looked as if it would settle down.

Hugh had problems, many of them financial, and Ida plunged back
into literary work. Before long she had five publishers, multiple pen-
names (including *Susan Barrie, Rose Burghley, Marguerite Bell, Avril Ives,*
and *Pamela Kent*) and readers spread across the world. With her family
she travelled widely, living in many parts of England and several
different countries, and also took to painting in oils. Later, in 2004, one
of her paintings was chosen for inclusion in a major national exhibition.

In 1971 Hugh died in Malta, and around the same time Ida took a
long introspective look at her career. A year or so earlier five of her
Regency novels had gained an enthusiastic response and so she turned
her attention to writing period fiction. She also moved to Cornwall
where many years later she died at the advanced age of 103, leaving
behind over a hundred highly successful novels. She is survived by her
daughter, Rosemary, also a novelist and who devoted herself to looking
after Ida for many years.

# TITLES BY IDA POLLOCK

### *as* **Joan Allen**
Indian Love
Palanquins & Coloured Lanterns

### *as* **Susan Barrie**
A Case of Heart Trouble
A Moment in Paris
Accidental Bride
Air Ticket
Bride-in-Waiting
Carpet of Dreams
Castle Thunderbird
Dear Tiberius
Four Roads to Windrush
Heart Specialist
Hotel Stardust
House of the Laird
Marry A Stranger
Master of Mellincourt
Mistress of Brown Furrows
Moon at the Full
Mountain Magic
Night of the Singing Birds
No Just Cause
Return to Tremarth
Rose in the Bud
Royal Purple
So Dear to my Heart
The Gates of Dawn
The Marriage Wheel
The Quiet Heart
The Stars of San Cecilio
The Wings of the Morning
Victoria and the Nightingale
Wild Sonata

### *as* **Jane Beaufort**
Dangerous Lover
Love in High Places
Nightingale in the Sycamore

### *as* **Marguerite Bell**
A Distant Drum
A Rose for Danger
Bride by Auction
Moonfire
Sea Change
The Devil's Daughter
The Runaway

### *as* **Rose Burghley**
A Quality of Magic
And be thy Love
Bride of Alaine
Highland Mist
Love in the Afternoon
an of Destiny
The Afterglow
The Bay of Moonlight
The Garden of Don Jose
The Sweet Surrender

### *as* **Anita Charles**
Autumn Wedding
Interlude for Love
My Heart at your Feet
One Coin in the Fountain
The Black Benedicts
The King of the Castle
The Moon & Bride's Hill
White Rose of Love

### *as* **Averil Ives**
Desire for the Star
Haven of the Heart
Island in the Dawn
Love in Sunlight
Master of Hearts
The Secret Heart
The Uncertain Glory

### *as* **Ida Pollock**
Country Air
Lady in Danger
Summer Conspiracy
The Gentle Masquerade
The Uneasy Alliance

### *as* **Barbara Rowan**
Flower for a Bride
Isle of Lost Magic
Love is Forever
Mountain of Dreams
Silver Fire
The Keys of the Castle

### *as* **Pamela Kent**
A Touch of Starlight
Beloved Enemies
Bladon`s Rock
Chateau of Fire
City of Palms
Cuckoo in the Night
Dawn on High Mountain
Desert Doorway
Desert Gold
Enemy Lover
Flight to the Stars
Gideon Faber's Chance
Journey in the Dark
Julie [Dawning Splendour]
Man from the Sea
Meet me in Istanbul
Moon over Africa
Nile Dusk
Star Creek
Sweet Barbary
The Man Who Came Back
The Night of Stars
White Heat

### *as* **Mary Whistler**
Enchanted Autumn
Escape to Happiness
Pathway of Roses
The Young Nightingales

# Moon Over
# Africa

*Ida Pollock*
*(Writing as Pamela Kent)*

HOUSE OF
STRATUS

This edition published in 2012 by House of Stratus, an imprint of
Stratus Books Ltd., Lisandra House, Fore Street,
Looe, Cornwall, PL13 1AD, U.K.
www.houseofstratus.com

Typeset by House of Stratus.

A catalogue record for this book is available from the British Library
and the Library of Congress.

ISBN 07551-4451-1
EAN 978-07551-4451-8

# Chapter One

Elizabeth was standing beside the rail watching with an absorbed look on her face as the ship drew slowly into Cape Town harbour.

In the way the memorable skyline of Manhattan comes upon you as you enter New York harbour, and lovely Malabar Hill proclaims Bombay, so Table Mountain provides a never-to-be-forgotten first impression of South Africa, and although Elizabeth had never seen New York, and she had certainly never been to India – this was, as a matter of fact, her first long journey outside her own country – she was prepared to believe that Table Mountain was the most impressive sight she would ever be permitted to witness.

Rising, as it does, sheer out of the sea, its flat top so often covered with a snowy tablecloth of billowing cloud, its massive rock and thickly wooded slopes display a dozen different colours, and at its foot straggles one of the loveliest cities in the world. Because of the mountain planted so solidly and inescapably in its midst, Cape Town finds it impossible to be compact, and its suburbs follow the coastline for miles, running up and down the green foothills at the base of Table Mountain. This cluster of seaside dwellings, with the unbelievably blue sea piling on to the golden beaches, awakes a feeling of breathless astonishment in the heart of every traveller, and Elizabeth was such an unseasoned one that in her case the astonishment was enough to fix her rigidly to the side of the ship, clinging to the teak handrail with fingers that, despite the lovely warmth of the morning, were a little cold with awe.

She thought of Devon and Cornwall, and the tiny coves and fishing villages she knew there. She thought of the golden width of sand on the north Cornish coast. But here all that was magnified a thousandfold, and her sensations as she gazed were a mixture of shivering excitement and impatience to be at last off the ship.

Around her there was a good deal of bustle and movement. People who were disembarking were making last-minute frantic searches of their cabins in order to be sure that they had left none of their personal possessions behind, and there were the usual farewells being said and addresses exchanged.

Elizabeth had made certain that all her possessions were securely stowed away in her baggage before breakfast that morning, and everything she had was ready to be shot through the Customs when the moment arrived. Owing to the fact that she was naturally almost painfully reserved she had not made so many friends during the voyage that it had taken her long to say goodbye to the few who sincerely wished to hear of her again, and now, in a crisp suit and little hat which sat well down on her soft gold hair – palest wedding-ring gold – she stood noticeably alone while others gushed and made wild promises around her.

But all at once a voice beside her made her start and turn, clutching her large white handbag.

"Journey's end, Miss Ransome?" said the voice. It was quiet and cool, and to Elizabeth it mocked slightly, as did the dark eyes with the strange little golden lights in them when she lifted her own and met their regard. "They do sometimes end in lovers' meetings, but I believe it's your father you're expecting to be met by, isn't it?"

Elizabeth nodded, unable to find her voice for a moment. Nigel Van Kane had addressed her on three separate occasions during the voyage, but she hardly felt that as a result of that they knew one another very well. He was a tall, spare, impeccably turned-out man in his middle thirties who looked well in a thin tussore suit – perhaps it was the contrast with his slightly swarthy skin, and his hair that was as sleek and black as an Indian's – and because he had been invited by the captain to sit at his table, and had occupied one of the most exclusive cabins on A Deck, he had been very popular during the voyage.

Certain seasoned travellers had obviously recognised him, and had vouched for him amongst the rest. There was the usual rich widow on board who had made a dead set at him, and quite a number of pretty girls had danced with him, and no doubt more than one of them had entertained secret hopes that the dances might lead to something else, for it was reported that he was one of the richest of the wine growers in the Cape Province area, and in addition he was that irresistibly attractive thing to an unmarried young woman, a bachelor who appeared unattached.

Elizabeth, with whom he had never once danced – although that set her apart in a unique position, for if not the prettiest girl on board, she was certainly very attractive, and despite her aloofness she loved dancing, and did not offer rebuffs when politely requested to act as a partner – would not have described him as a handsome man. But there was something about him which even she, who had had little opportunity to get to know him, recognised as more forceful and vital than mere masculine good looks. Certainly more magnetic.

For instance, if he was standing several paces away, and she had her back to him, she was almost certain to feel his presence, and to turn as if compelled as soon as she became aware of him – or she would have done so until today, when she was absorbed in the thought of going ashore.

But apart from that first night, when she was leaving the dining saloon after dinner and he had stopped her and asked her if she was Elizabeth Ransome, and told her that he knew her father, their interchanges had been strictly limited. Others must have noticed that he didn't actually avoid her, but he never seemed to have any time for her. It was true that he was much sought after himself, but there were moments when it would have been the merest form of politeness to drop down into a vacant chair beside her and ask her whether she was enjoying the voyage, or bring up the subject of her father which he had introduced himself.

One night when a dance was in progress she was the only young woman of her generation sitting alone on the fringe of the dancers, and he was standing smoking a cigarette on the other side of the floor, but he still did not ask her to dance.

She had felt the somewhat surprised looks of one or two of the older women as he passed close to her on his way to seek a breath of air on deck, and she had flushed slightly because all in a moment she had felt that there was something wrong with her. There must be something wrong. She was wearing her prettiest evening dress, a delicate white cotton printed with palest pink roses, which matched the banners of pink in her clear cheeks. But apparently he hadn't even noticed that she looked conscious of her aloneness there on the edge of the floor, and if he had it had obviously left him quite unmoved.

For the first time in her life she had felt as if she had received a deliberate snub.

Sometimes in the dining saloon she had caught him watching her, and once when she was sitting reading on deck she had looked up to discover that he was observing her from a position near the rail, where he was all but surrounded by a bevy of beauty. But there had been nothing suggestive of friendliness or interest in his look, and it had even surprised her a little, because it had struck her as faintly hostile. And when he saw that she was looking back at him the hostility gave place to that odd look of mockery which could so easily have been imagined, but which nevertheless managed to distort his mouth slightly as he curtly inclined his head.

Sometimes she wondered how much he knew about her and her life, and about the life of her father and mother. Did he know that her parents had been separated since she was twelve? And as she was now twenty-two that meant that she had not seen her father for ten years! Ten years during which they had corresponded, and he had never forgotten her birthdays, or omitted to send her a present at Christmas-time. Kay and Christine, her two elder sisters – the one a highly successful model, and the other becoming known for the exquisite miniatures she painted – had thought it all rather amusing and pathetic, because their little sister seemed determined to cling on to the fact that she *had* a father, even though he was not a very satisfactory one.

And, as Mrs. Ransome pointed out to her friends, with that hurt look on her face that Elizabeth had grown up to recognise the instant it appeared, a father who preferred medical missions and disease-ridden corners of the globe, horrible insects and squalor, nature in the raw and impossible climatic conditions, to a very nice family of three daughters *and* a wife who, even after all her trials and troubles, still looked almost as young as the girl he had married, was hardly the sort of father one would call ideal!

All her friends pitied Mrs. Ransome, and not one of them had a good word to spare for Dr. Ransome. There had been a time when she was still in her very early teens when this constant condemnation had irked Elizabeth, and it had even affected very slightly her feelings towards her mother, who looked nowadays like a somewhat faded copy of Kay when she was at her most glamorous. She had strongly suspected that her mother traded on that fragile Dresden china appearance of hers, her declared inability to "cope" with three great girls growing up around her, and only just a very small allowance …!

Elizabeth had even suspected that the allowance was not so very small, either. Anyway, it had permitted them to live quite comfortably in a very nice house in one of the outer suburbs of London, where they had a good garden, good clothes, and all the essentials of life. And she and her sisters had been given quite reasonably good educations.

But sometimes her father's letters – which none of the others even bothered to read – had breathed, she thought, a kind of loneliness … He gave her few details of his actual daily life, but he painted her pictures of colour and warmth which charmed her. There must be magic in Africa, she thought, even in Central Africa. Then he wrote to her about Ghana, provided her with an address in Zaire, and moved southward to Rhodesia. After a period of illness – she did not know that it had been critical illness – he went farther south still, and it was from Cape Town that she began to receive letters. And finally it seemed that he had taken root on a little fruit farm where, from the almost contented tone of his correspondence, he was experiencing the satisfaction of living amongst growing things, and feeling much better in health.

Elizabeth felt sometimes that she longed to see him, and she made up her mind that she would see him when her Aunt Jane died suddenly and left her two thousand pounds with which she could more or less do as she liked. She gave her mother two hundred pounds of this unexpected wealth, and split another two hundred equally between Kay and Christine, and with the remaining sixteen hundred she bought herself an outfit and a cruise ticket to South Africa.

Her closest relatives thought this was merely a whim, but they didn't really do anything to dissuade her. Perhaps they knew it wouldn't be any use, for of the three children about whom he knew so little, Dr. Ransome's youngest child was the most like him. She was the type to get the bit between her teeth and hang on to it. Not fierce or stubborn, but merely determined when it came to something which lay close to her heart.

And now here she was at the end of her voyage, and the ship was making its stately progress into harbour. In a very short while now she would see her father, and a short while after that …

When Nigel Van Kane spoke her name at her elbow she was so occupied with her thoughts that for a few moments she could only stare at him rather stupidly, and then she flushed and became self-conscious. Surely he didn't think it necessary to say goodbye to her, she thought, when for more than a fortnight they had remained practically strangers?

Then all at once she noticed that he had an open telegram in his hand – a lean brown hand which looked even browner by contrast with his immaculate shirt-cuff – and he was holding it out towards her. The smiling derisiveness on his eyes filled her with an inclination to shrink back against the rail.

"I hope this isn't going to be a tremendous disappointment to you," he said, "but after all you are not to be met by your father. He can't possibly manage it. But he has wired me and asked me to look after you in his stead, and I am to deliver you to him if you have no serious objections?'

## Chapter Two

The disappointment which descended on Elizabeth was so great that in the first few moments she felt like a child who was to be deprived of a treat to which it had looked forward for weeks. She said: "Oh, no!" involuntarily, and then clapped a hand to her lips as if the realisation that this might appear to him as rude struck her almost as keenly as her disappointment.

"I'm afraid it's 'Oh, yes'!" he replied, looking down at her from his superior height and confusing her still more because the suspicion of a smile on his lips took on a distinctly bleak curve. "Unless, of course, you'd prefer to tell me to go about my own business, and feel confident of seeing yourself through the Customs, and so forth? You're not likely to run into any language difficulties, and you're not exactly an infant, so you can do as you wish. But please let me know what you do wish."

Elizabeth felt the hot colour rush up over her face and neck, and although he was still holding out the telegram she was so mesmerised by his look that she could only continue to gaze back at him fixedly, her grey eyes pleading with him for more information.

"I'm afraid I—I don't understand," she stammered. "Is my father ill?"

He tucked the telegram between two of her nerveless fingers, and recommended that she made herself familiar with its contents. The lines of type were inclined to blur before her eyes, especially in the bright sunshine, but even so she gathered this much: "... grateful if you would contact Elizabeth. Explain unable to meet. Feel sure can safely leave her to you ..."

"But—but why you?" Elizabeth managed to ask at last in bewilderment.

"Why not me?" She was quite sure now that she had never seen such a hard and ruthless face before in her life, and there was also something slightly forbidding about it. The lips were thin and beautifully shaped, but they were also cruel and cynical, and his chin jutted noticeably, and had a rock-like pugnacity about it. And those strange dark eyes of his, with the little darting flames which leapt up and down and mocked and derided continually – they made her feel almost afraid. No wonder no woman had managed to secure him during this voyage – or at least, judging by the disappointed looks of the rich widow, and the pretty girls who had danced with him, and danced attendance on him, and who had had to say their farewells to him the night before, he had merely been amusing himself when there was no other amusement to be had, and was not even contrite about damaging a few hearts.

"I—I didn't know you knew my father well enough ..."

"But since I do, and since he considers me respectable enough to take charge of you, are you also prepared to take the risk?" There was a note of cold impatience in his voice this time which warned her that if she showed any further hesitation he was quite capable of turning on his heel and leaving her there on the deck, so she said quickly: "I'm sorry if I seem rather stupid, but I wasn't expecting anything like this to happen. And I—I've been looking forward—" She broke off. "It's very kind of you to be willing to be bothered with me."

"Not at all. But if we're going ashore we'd better not waste any more time." He touched her arm with the tips of his strong brown fingers and propelled her forward along the deck. "I suppose all your luggage is out of your cabin, and there's nothing more to collect?"

"No. I assembled everything. I—I don't think I've left anything behind."

"You probably have," he said, a little sneeringly, "even if it's only a pocket handkerchief! Women are good at that sort of thing."

Elizabeth remained silent, but she was quite sure that even if she had left a diamond-studded wrist watch behind in her cabin she would never have found the courage to request permission to return for it while that compelling touch was on her arm.

But despite the terseness of his speech, and the feeling which he communicated that he was deriving no pleasure from having her under his wing, the speed with which they got through the Customs and won free from all the last-minute entanglements of the voyage to hail a taxi and leave the dock area behind them was considerably greater than that which Elizabeth would have achieved alone. And the sensation of confidence which having a man at her elbow who could order the disposition of the luggage, and give instructions concerning an hotel to the taxi-man, imparted to her was sufficient to counteract the sensation of obligation which she had been certain would be intolerable at first, and she found herself uttering grateful thanks when at last they were inside the taxi.

"I wouldn't have known quite what to do or where to go," she confessed, "if my father hadn't sent that telegram. In fact, I should have felt very lost. But I still can't see very clearly why you should have to put yourself out to look after me, Mr. Van Kane."

He ignored the last part of her speech.

"Naturally your father would not allow a young woman of your age to arrive in a strange country without making some arrangements for her to be met," he said, in a quiet but incisive drawl, "if he couldn't be at the docks himself. I've known Dr. Ransome for a number of years, and whatever happened he wouldn't have failed you."

Elizabeth felt about twelve, instead of twenty-two, but she was aware that a great many people thought she did not look nearly her age, and the light coating of tan she had acquired during the voyage, the youthful simplicity of her linen suit, in a delicate shade of cool lime-green which emphasised the light gold of her hair, probably made her look younger still.

"And you happened to be making the voyage in the *Star of the South* at the same time as myself. That was strange," she observed, stealing a sideways glance at him. "For me it was also convenient."

"Fate taking a hand in your affairs!" he remarked, without so much as a smile curving his lips, or even a hint of irony in his eyes.

"But it doesn't strike me as particularly strange that we should be travelling in the same ship, for even a South African does sometimes visit England, and naturally he has to return."

"Y—yes," she stammered rather awkwardly, "of course."

But she could have added that what did strike her as strange was the fact that, while they were travelling in the same ship, he had deliberately gone out of his way to avoid her—although he apparently thought well of her father!—and now that she was more or less thrust on him he expected her to accept it as natural. That and his ill-concealed impatience, and his tendency to be almost rude at times!

She lay back against the seat and looked out of the window at Cape Town as they sped through it, after leaving the docks behind them. They were moving quickly along Adderley Street, which runs straight from the docks to the more dignified corners of the great city, and is the spine from which the ribs of the city spring. In the warm air everything seemed to shimmer, including the pink bricks of the House of Representatives, and the foliage of the oak trees which all but surrounded it. The colourful crowds on the pavements dazzled her eyes, and the sun was so golden, falling from a width of blue sky such as she had never seen before in her life, that it almost hurt her eyes.

"Of course, I suppose I could have hired a car to take me out to my father," she said suddenly, just before they drew up outside the hotel. "It's only a distance of fourteen or fifteen miles or so, according to his letters. And that would have been the obvious thing to do."

"But on the whole I'm rather glad things turned out this way," Nigel Van Kane surprised her considerably by replying rather bluntly, and then a coal-black porter in a dazzling white uniform had fallen upon their joint luggage, and the impressive façade of an extremely dignified hotel was looming up right in front of them.

Elizabeth looked hesitatingly at the front of the hotel, and at the sight of her new suitcases being carried inside it she felt concerned at the cost which this might result in. But Van Kane took her arm again almost peremptorily, and within a few moments they were inside the foyer, and she was standing before a reception desk, while her companion addressed a few words to the obsequious clerk who was standing behind it.

After the blinding glare outside, the hum of the traffic, and the babel of various noises, the dimness and the silence which prevailed in this handsomely equipped entrance to an old-established hotel of the five-star variety reminded Elizabeth of the dimness and silence of a church. But she was glad of the coolness and the quiet, and when her companion turned to her, and looked her up and down for a moment, she wondered whether there was anything wrong with her appearance which was at odds with the excessive dignity of such surroundings.

But he merely said quietly: "I've booked you a room, so you can go upstairs and have a wash and titivate yourself if you want to. I've some business which I must attend to before lunch, but I'll be back in good time, so perhaps you'll wait for me down below here?"

"Oh, but—" Elizabeth began. She wanted to protest that it was hardly necessary to book a room if they were leaving before it would be possible to occupy it for a night. But, as if he read her thoughts, and gathered that she was shrinking from the prospect of incurring expense, he said with a cold, almost a sarcastic curl to his lips which brought a hot blush to her cheeks and made her feel almost as if she was blushing all over: "Don't worry about the room! Your father will make himself responsible for that."

Elizabeth turned silently away from him and moved in the direction of the lift gates, which were being held open for her by a smartly uniformed liftboy. She felt in that moment that under no circumstances could she ever possibly like this man who seemed to be taking a kind of keen delight in making her feel small and rather awkward, and who obviously had an extraordinarily poor opinion of her.

But why, she asked herself, why ...? When he knew next to nothing about her!

Upstairs in the luxurious bedroom which had been reserved for her, with its plush carpet and its mirrors, she was glad of the opportunity to do what had been suggested, however, and after a refreshing wash and a re-application of make-up she felt better, and more able to do battle – if battle was going to be demanded of her during lunch!

She was not looking forward to that lunch with Nigel Van Kane. She wondered what it was about him that made her father obviously trust him enough – and have sufficient confidence in him to be sure that a favour would not be ignored – to wish him to take temporary charge of his daughter, and she wished in her innermost heart that almost anyone else had been selected to execute the trust. Although it was true that it took all kinds to make a world, and that people did sometimes improve on acquaintance, she felt that a world peopled by hard, resistant types like the swarthy-featured Van Kane, with his mocking dark eyes, would be a very unpleasant world indeed; and as to his improving on acquaintance—!

Well, that was something she could not envisage ever coming to pass.

It was true that he had been popular on the boat, but possibly the atmosphere of a liner, and careless souls determined to have a good time and see only the best side of everyone, had worked a miracle. Or, possibly, it was only he and she who were mutually antagonistic to one another, and in that case they would remain antagonistic, which made the thought of the lunch room more like a shadow than ever.

He was waiting for her when she descended to the ground floor of the hotel, and he looked very tall and commanding in his faultlessly tailored light silk suit. A man with something about him, she had to admit, which might cause some people to turn and look after him if they passed him in the street. But to her it was his arrogance which was the most noticeable thing about him – that and his quiet, somewhat forbidding air of strength and determination, which stamped an implacable look on his features.

Elizabeth had added an extra touch of lipstick to her lips, and because the heat and the excitement of landing had made her look rather more pale than usual, their soft shape was particularly noticeable. Her eyes were innocent of any sort of attempt to improve their dove-like greyness, and the fine gold eyebrows which swept above repeated the light dusting of gold at the tips of her eyelashes.

In the V-shaped neck of the cool lime suit the creamy base of her rounded throat was embellished by a tiny gold cross, which depended from a neat row of seed pearls. Otherwise she wore no adornment of any kind, and her slim fingers and wrists were innocent of either rings or bracelets, although the fingers were particularly well kept, the oval nails pink like the inside of a shell.

Nigel Van Kane's eyes were on her when, having been bowed to a table by an attentive waiter, they sat down facing one another. For an instant, she thought, there was a glimmer of something like puzzlement in the eyes with the little gold lights in them as they studied her, but if there was it vanished so rapidly that she became sure she had made a mistake. He picked up a menu and passed it to her.

"Order what you want," he said. "The food here is quite good."

Elizabeth could believe that. The dining room was positively sumptuous, and the menu, when she looked at it, bewildered her by offering her a diversity of dishes she knew nothing about. In the end she followed Van Kane's example and chose an iced soup, cold turkey and salad, and an apple flan with meringue.

It was towards the end of the meal that the man opposite her said suddenly: "How old were you when you last saw your father?"

"I was twelve." She looked up at him with wide, surprised eyes.

A cold, cynical expression settled round his mouth.

"That's not much of an age, is it? And children soon forget."

"But I wasn't a child, and I haven't forgotten!" There was indignation in her voice.

"Haven't you?"

"No."

"Then possibly your mother and your sisters have forgotten? Possibly they are no longer interested in the possession of a husband, or a father?"

This was so true that Elizabeth could only stare down at the slice of flan that was placed in front of her, and she felt an almost painful embarrassment, because however much she might wish to do so she could not deny such an accusation as this. Why, her mother openly boasted to her friends that since her marriage had proved rather pointless she had decided to forget all about it!

"What made you decide to come out to Africa?" Van Kane inquired abruptly.

Elizabeth explained about the legacy and her desire to see her father again – this was said almost defensively in view of what she knew her closest relatives felt – and although the cold look stayed round his mouth she thought that his eyes grew more amused.

"A little flutter, eh? A taste of the world before you settle down and marry someone nice and dependable in England! No doubt your mother will see to it that you marry wisely and well when the time comes in view of her own unfortunate experience! But what I would like to know, if you won't think me impertinent for wishing for some enlightenment on this head, is what would you have done if no one had left you a legacy? Would you have made any attempt at all to come out here and see your father, or would you have decided that the wisest thing would be to forget about him altogether? Oh, I know that you've written to him at quite regular intervals throughout all these years"—surveying her strangely—"but you probably thought it was romantic to correspond with a father who was living in a place like Africa, even though he had to cope with all sorts of filthy diseases and things like that that you wouldn't want to come into close contact with – naturally ..."

His quiet drawl made her stare back at him with the sudden feeling that the hostility she had sensed – the contempt, even – was now much nearer the surface, and she said quietly: "I would have come out to him much sooner if I had been able to afford the passage money."

An inscrutable smile chased itself across his lips.

"Perhaps you thought that being your father he should send you your passage money?"

"I have no idea whether he could afford it."

"No?" One of his dark eyebrows lifted itself slightly above its fellow. "No idea whether he's prosperous or otherwise?"

Elizabeth shook her head.

"He has never discussed his affairs in letters, and all that I know is that he seems to be quite happy now that he's fruit farming, and that the farm itself is called Groote Kloof, which means Great Valley. It doesn't matter to me whether he's prosperous or not, but I see no reason why he shouldn't be reasonably prosperous. For his sake I hope that he is."

"Very filial, I'm sure." There seemed to be a dark sparkle of humour in his eyes, and he summoned the waiter and ordered him to bring their coffee. "But your mother's interest in your father's financial concerns must be considerably greater than your own. She probably enquires into them occasionally?" he suggested.

"I don't think she has ever done so," Elizabeth told him, and this time both of Nigel Van Kane's eyebrows shot upwards.

"Then that almost certainly explains something," he said.

Elizabeth had a vague feeling at heart which was not a pleasant one, for ever since the meal had started and he had begun his determined questioning she had begun to be aware of something – she was not quite sure what it was – but it weighed upon her like apprehension. And, in any case, what was all this to do with Nigel Van Kane, and what right had he to question her at all? She ignored the liqueur he had ordered for her, which was glowing like green fire at her elbow, and looked at him across the table, her grey eyes wide and perturbed and suddenly almost challenging.

"You seem to know a lot about my father and his affairs," she said. "You even know that I've written to him quite regularly for a number of years. Perhaps you also know"—she paused—"why it was that he couldn't meet me today?"

An annoyingly cool smile answered her.

"I have had no direct communication with him since I left England."

"Apart from the telegram you received today?"

"Apart from that telegram."

"But you—you did hear from him before you left England?"

"Well?" he suggested, over the glowing end of a cigarette he had just lighted.

"Was he—was he well when you heard from him last?"

"As well as he has been since his Central African days."

"Then he's not particularly fit nowadays? Is that what you mean?"

Her voice was anxious, and her eyes were anxious, but all that he offered her by way of reassurance as he answered was contained in a curt: "Dr. Ransome's health has not been good for years now, but as you've managed to survive quite well without making exhaustive inquiries concerning it for the same number of years I wouldn't allow myself to become agitated about it now if I were you. In an hour or so you will see him and be able to decide for yourself whether his condition is what you imagined it to be. And in the meantime, if you'll occupy yourself in the lounge – having tea or something – I'll pick you up about four o'clock and drive you out to Groote Kloof which – as you so knowledgeably informed me – means Great Valley!"

With a mocking, humiliating smile he rose and accompanied her back to the lounge, and then she watched his tall figure disappearing arrogantly through the swing doors in the direction of the foyer.

# Chapter Three

As the road sweeps upward out of Cape Town there is a superb view of the bay. At four o'clock in the afternoon the light lay on it almost blindly, and the far-off mountains rose against the sky in a flat wash of violet and blue. To Elizabeth it was an astonishing thing to see arum lilies bordering the way in early November; and the sight of hollyhocks and dahlias – flowers which she had believed belonged exclusively to England – blooming side by side with bougainvillea and hibiscus in gardens that were swiftly passed astonished her still further.

Not that she allowed surprise to show in her face, or revealed the fact that she was even particularly interested in the colourful prospect on either hand, as she sat as if quietly withdrawn into herself in the seat beside the wheel of Nigel Van Kane's powerful dust-coloured car. He had obviously collected the car from a garage when he left her after lunch, and now his thin brown hands rested purposefully on the wheel, and his dark eyes scanned the road ahead as they proceeded in the direction of Groote Kloof.

Just as Elizabeth appeared to have no wish to enter into conversation, so he, too, sat silent, only drawing her attention to the university, a dream of Rhodes, magnificently sited against the massive slopes of the Devil's Peak, which soared up into the blue sky, when they passed it. And he also indicated an enclosure behind which zebra and buck were grazing.

For an instant some of the excitement which had attacked Elizabeth early that morning when she had caught her first glimpse of Cape Town from the deck of the *Star of the South* swept over her again. And the breathless thought intruded that this was indeed Africa! And whatever happened from now on she had actually set foot in this fabulous country, and was seeing animals that she had hitherto only seen in the confines of the London Zoo in their more or less natural state, and splashes of such brilliant colour that her eyes ached from the assault upon them, although she yearned to go on seeing more.

And then the excitement died as she glanced at the man beside her. He had filled her with apprehension and a strange feeling of foreboding – a feeling that the miles which still lay between her and her father could not be swallowed up fast enough by the wheels of this expensive car (which, incidentally, was exactly the sort of car she would have expected a man of Nigel Van Kane's obviously exclusive tastes, and equally obvious ability to pander to them, to possess). She was anxious to assure herself that there really was nothing seriously wrong with his health, and that this holiday on which she had set so much store, and which was to bring them together again for the first time since their parting when she was twelve, would be all that she had hoped and dreamed it would be. Something memorable which she could treasure in after years.

But Nigel Van Kane had given her a nasty cold little feeling inside, despite the brilliant warmth that was all about them, and she wished with all her heart that if he had had to make the trip back to South Africa he had chosen a ship in which she was not travelling herself, and that her father had never known anything about him. She could have managed quite well, once she had landed, without any assistance from anyone, and she could certainly have dispensed with the assistance she was receiving from Van Kane. He had given her a most disagreeable lunch—if one excluded the edible part of it!—and now she felt that his eyes were occasionally glancing sideways at her, when he was not too preoccupied with his driving, and that there was a strange curve on the lips of the sphinx.

He knew, she thought, that her hands were tightly and almost nervously clenched together in her lap, and that she was longing for the end of the journey. He knew, but he was not the type to spare her any sympathy, or to wish to make things easier for her. He was content to remain silent and detached behind the wheel of his car, while her imagination worked overtime and was beginning to torture her.

When they were within a mile of their destination he told her so. Elizabeth felt her heart do a kind of wild and frightened leap, and she peered fixedly ahead. For what was a mile to a car that ate up miles like a hungry demon? In a minute or so she would be there …!

In other circumstances she would have been enchanted by the beauty of the scenery that was now opening up on either hand. Scenery that reminded her a little of the South of France, for there were vineyards climbing the slopes, and thick ridges of fir trees rising against the wall of mountains that enclosed them on the north. There was a new touch of mellowness to the light of the sun, too, as it slipped westwards, and when a white house came in sight – a house that might have been a white chateau on a hillside in France, and protected by age-old trees – it appeared to be bathed in something tender and transforming that stamped the pattern of motionless leaves on the white walls, like a pattern of intricate lace. And in front of it were green lawns, and beds of flowers – masses and masses of brilliant flowers. And there was a winding drive which led up to it, and the house itself had steep gables, and a pillared stoep looking out to the mountains.

Impossible to believe that lions and leopards had at one time haunted such a district as this, and visited such a house as this – just as impossible as it was to believe that anything so spacious and gracious and dignified had been acquired by her father!

It was not the sort of house she had pictured him living in. In her imagination she had conjured up the outlines of something far more primitive.

But Van Kane had turned the car in at the approaches to the residence, and they were sweeping up the drive. Elizabeth looked at him in a certain amount of amazement, but he did not even look sideways at her. He brought the car to rest in front of the stoep, and Elizabeth descended when he held the door open for her. She could have sworn that his eyes mocked when he saw how uneasy and uncertain she looked, but she was peering into the shadows at the far end of the stoep, where, in a long cane chair, a white-haired figure was reclining. He had a light rug over his knees, despite the warmth, and there was a book in his blue-veined hands. He laid down the book and attempted to rise to his feet as Elizabeth moved forward, but Nigel Van Kane went quickly to him and prevented him, a strong persuasive hand upon his shoulder.

"No need to get up," he said, in a surprisingly gentle voice. "Elizabeth is here, and she can come to you!"

Elizabeth felt shocked and appalled, as if she was rooted suddenly to the floor of the veranda. She recognised Dr. Ransome at once, although it was ten years since they had come face to face, but never in her wildest dreams had she imagined that when she saw him again he would look like this.

He appeared to her to be shrunken, instead of tall and virile as she remembered him. His face was merely a bone structure with a delicate parchment-like skin stretched tightly over it, and his eyes seemed to have retreated into deep caverns. But even so, they were alert grey eyes, and at the first sight of Elizabeth a beam of happiness lit them from within, and a kind of luminous pleasure overspread his entire face.

"My dear!" he said. "It's good to see you!"

Elizabeth still felt as if her feet were all at once weighted with lead, and the messages dispatched by her brain urging her to go forward without hesitation and fling herself down at her father's feet simply could not be obeyed because she was bereft of the power to carry them out. She felt, rather than saw, Van Kane's eyes watching her – observing her reactions to this curiously shattering moment as if, behind the tight, cold mask of his face, a sensation of the most acute pleasure—almost an unholy pleasure!—had him in its grip. He was delighted to see her overcome like this, and so far as he was concerned she must struggle upwards through the shock of it alone, without any assistance from anyone or anything save the appeal in her father's eyes.

For Dr. Ransome's eyes were beginning to appeal to her to come nearer.

"Father," she exclaimed at last, "Father, I—!"

And then all at once she had subsided somehow into the seat beside him, and he was gripping her hands and holding them with surprising strength considering his fragile appearance, and gazing at her.

"Elizabeth, my dear," he told her, "you've grown out of all knowledge, but it's the most wonderful thing to have you here! I've been counting the days, I can and do assure you! But I'm sorry I was unable to meet you when your ship docked. However, I expect Nigel has explained everything to you, and you appreciate how much we have to be grateful to him for? He's perfectly willing that you shall remain here as a guest for as long as you want – as long as you can spare the time."

Elizabeth's eyes had widened so much that the golden-tipped eyelashes looked like golden-tipped reeds bending backwards from the blank grey surface of a lake.

"A g—guest?" she stammered.

"Yes, darling." Her father's eyes caressed her, and then he smiled a little – a faintly wry smile. "It must have struck you at once that Groote Kloof is not the sort of place *I* would ever be likely to own! And I think I explained to you in a letter"—hazily—"that material success and I have never had anything to do with one another, and that's why I've become a sort of pensioner of Nigel's. But he always makes me feel as if I've a genuine claim on him, which of course I haven't."

The explanation was so simply and gratefully given – with an upward look of deep affection at the man who stood silently regarding them both – that it was even more disturbing to Elizabeth than if some justification had been more wordily sought for to let her in on an arrangement which, however much it had been wrapped up in explanation, would have shocked her to the very core of her being.

Her father a pensioner of Nigel Van Kane's! Nigel Van Kane who, as she now realised with icy cold clarity of mind, had detested the very sight of her on the voyage! And if her mother and her two sisters had travelled with her he would probably have loathed them just as much, for he regarded the four of them as a complete let-down to her father, something with which he should never have been burdened, useless appendages who thought only of themselves, and in ten years had never seriously wasted one moment of even mildly concerned thought on the man who, however much he had to do without himself, had always provided for them!

It was a bitterly humiliating thought now that it smote her at last, and as she lifted her eyes dully to her host's face Elizabeth knew exactly what he was thinking. He was almost gloating over her discomfiture, smiling quietly with grim, unsympathetic eyes.

# Chapter Four

Outside the lawn was emerald in the last of the light, before the swift downward rush of the night. There were flaming beds of cannas and roses in full flower, aromatic shrubs, and some great tall trees which had probably stood where they were for a century and more, with the pale blue riven ridges of the mountains behind them soaring upwards into an arc of deeper blue sky.

Elizabeth had been brushing her hair while she looked out of the window, but now she turned and put the brush down on the dressing-table. It was a dressing-table which stood in a petticoat of highly glazed chintz – little pink rosebuds and delicate blue harebells on a clear green ground. The window curtains were of the same chintz, but the bedspread was clear green, and so were the rugs on the golden polished floor. There was a commodious wardrobe in light wood, and a bedside table on which stood a bedside lamp and a couple of new-looking novels.

Quite a pleasant bedroom, if a trifle bare. But there was a coolness about it at this hour, and the sweetness of the cannas came in at the windows, and the view from each of the windows was enough to tempt anyone to simply stand before them and just gaze and gaze.

Elizabeth, after she had unpacked her things and stowed them away in the wardrobe and the chest of drawers, had gazed for so long, rather blindly, that she was not even yet aware of all that she had gazed upon. She felt as if some screen had come down between her outer eye and her inner eye, and she was incapable just then of appreciating anything whatsoever, or even of feeling anything very much. She knew that inside her she felt rather cold, and her fingers were fumbling and none too steady when she wielded her hairbrush.

There came a light tap at the door, and a large, big-boned woman with hair which had been a very bright red but was now turning grey, small, shrewd blue eyes and a lot of freckles, wearing a dark dress with a bunch of keys attached to the belt, came in with a tray supporting a glass of something which looked like sherry, and a plate of biscuits.

"The master said he thought you'd probably be glad of a little refreshment to buck you up after your long day," she said, her accent so unmistakably the accent of the Scottish Highlands that Elizabeth stared. A broad smile answered her. "I'm Master Nigel's housekeeper, and the name's McClegg. I've been with him for years, so there's not much about him that I don't know!"—the smile expanding still further.

"And you come from Scotland?" Elizabeth said, because she felt that she must say something.

"No, dearie, I've never been to Scotland in my life, but my mother was a guid Scot—the name was MacTavish!—and McClegg hailed from Glasgow. But the poor man passed on five years ago, and that's why nowadays I keep house for Master Nigel. But I began by being his nurse!"

"I see," Elizabeth murmured, and she thought that Mrs. McClegg was extraordinarily well preserved considering that her employer must be somewhere in the neighbourhood of thirty or thirty-five himself.

The housekeeper set the glass of sherry down on the dressing-table top and looked keenly at Elizabeth.

"You do look a bit palish, dearie," she said. "Was it a shock finding your father in such poor shape, poor man? He had one of his turns about a week ago, and he hasn't picked up since. But maybe now that you've come he'll begin to brighten up."

"Yes; perhaps he will," Elizabeth muttered to her reflection in the mirror. She did look as if all the colour had fled away out of her face, she realised, and her eyes had a dull, wounded look in them – so different from the bright sparkle with which they had greeted the first sight of Table Mountain only that morning. "Does he often—is he often like this?" she asked. "I mean, are his bad turns fairly frequent?"

"Well, yes, I'm afraid they are getting rather more frequent," Mrs. McClegg admitted. "It's his heart, you know – it won't stand up to any sort of strain nowadays, and excitement isn't really good for him either. And I expect he was excited at the thought of your coming."

"It's a thousand pities I didn't come much, much earlier!" Elizabeth cried in her heart, as she turned and groped in her wardrobe for a dress that would be suitable to wear for the evening. She had no idea whom she would be meeting at dinner, or whether perhaps she would be dining alone since her father had already been settled down for the night in his room, but searching for something to wear occupied her hands and kept her face averted from those shrewd, bright eyes of Mrs. McClegg's, which sometimes, she felt certain, saw more than it was always desirable they should see.

"If you don't feel up to making an effort," the housekeeper suggested, "I could bring a tray to your room? Then you could slip along and say good night to your father, and go to bed early."

For one instant Elizabeth saw a mental picture of Nigel Van Kane's face when the information was conveyed to him that Miss Elizabeth Ransome felt too exhausted to appear at dinner, and the derisive sparkle which she felt certain would light his dark eyes made her shake her head hastily.

"No, thank you, Mrs. McClegg. It's good of you to suggest it, but I shall be quite all right – quite all right!" she repeated. "It's just that I was up rather early this morning, and—and seeing my father looking so ill did upset me a bit."

"Of course, dearie." Mrs. McClegg sounded comfortably understanding. "But don't think that Mr. Nigel would mind a scrap if you stayed in your room. As a matter of fact, he's not particularly sociable, and he'll probably be going off somewhere after dinner, and may be in a bit of a rush to get it over. His trip to England, you know – there are one or two friends he may be anxious to see, and I'm very certain they're more than anxious to see him!"—with a sudden slight tightening of her lips, and a knowing look in her eyes.

"All the same, I think it would look better if I went down to dinner," Elizabeth said, and the housekeeper nodded her head.

"Very well, my dear. I'll run a bath for you. But don't forget to drink this," indicating the sherry.

Elizabeth picked it up and sipped at it, but when she was alone she gazed at it thoughtfully. She could hardly believe that the man whose antipathy towards her she felt was almost a living thing had bothered to concern himself with her need for some sort of a stimulant after the gruelling half-hour she had been forced to endure downstairs on the wide stoep after her arrival at Groote Kloof.

Even now, when it was safely behind her, the thought of that half-hour made her feel curiously weak, as if all her vitality had been remorselessly drained away from her, and had left her curiously limp and quite unlike her normal self. To begin with, there had been the shock of discovering that Dr. Ransome was – or seemed to be – a more or less doomed man; and on top of that the second shock of discovering that he was apparently entirely dependent on the generosity of Nigel Van Kane, while his wife and family had known nothing about it, had proved almost more than she could take in one afternoon.

She had had to make a supreme effort to put up some sort of a pretence for her father's sake, but while tea had been served to them, and she had had to do the honours of the tea-table, the mortification she had experienced, the hot resentment because she had never been warned—not even how seriously ill her father was!—had done something to her which she felt could never be undone, and which was almost as bad as a profound shock to her entire nervous system.

Her hands had shaken while she manipulated the tea things, and at the back of her eyes there had been scalding tears because her heart was ravaged by the sight of Dr. Ransome. And she had had to make light small talk for the latter's benefit, giving him information about the past two weeks, and all the little details of the voyage – wondering while she did so what he would think if she added the surprising item that his patron had not even asked her to dance when she sat alone on the fringe of a dance floor, and he had stood opposite her and ignored her and smoked a cigarette! And tried to make it all sound interesting and exciting, which indeed it had been until that morning had dawned!

Less than twelve hours, and yet how changed she felt since this time yesterday! Dr. Ransome had not asked her about her mother or her sisters or her home life, but she felt that that would come later on when they were alone. But his eyes had remained avidly glued to her face, and there had been a hectic pink flush in his cheeks when at last the half-hour was over and the host himself had helped him to his room, with the assistance of a tall, widely smiling, dark-skinned youth in immaculate white, who had handled him and regarded him with the gentleness and concern of a woman.

Elizabeth saw Van Kane's eyes rest intently for a few moments on that flush in the invalid's cheeks before he persuaded him to return to his room, and when he returned to the stoep she was not altogether surprised by the stony, accusing look he cast at her.

"If you take my advice you will let him rest tonight, and, not excite him any further than you have done by your arrival," he said. There was nothing but cold criticism in his tone. "As you can see for yourself, he is very frail, and excitement is not good for him."

"Why didn't you let me know?" Elizabeth's voice was almost as hard and as stony as his own.

"Why?" He looked at her disdainfully. "Would it have made any different if you had known? If you hadn't had that legacy left you, and you had been informed that he was ill, would you have made a superhuman effort to raise the funds and come out here and see him? Would your mother have done so, or your sisters?"

Elizabeth turned away. She felt it was useless to put up any defence for herself and her family at that moment, and her gesture of wishing to ignore such a question obviously incensed him. He called loudly, and the black servant Muemba returned and was instructed to show her to her room, to which her luggage had already been conveyed. Without another word, and without looking at him, Elizabeth followed stiffly after the servant.

When she was dressed to go downstairs to dinner she felt, for a moment, almost afraid to leave the sanctuary of her own room. This was a hostile house – or, at any rate, its owner was hostile towards her, and although it was a beautiful house, after the style of the old Cape Dutch houses she had sometimes read about, it was not in the least the sort of house she had expected to find herself in twelve hours after bidding goodbye to the *Star of the South*.

When she did at last leave her room behind her she was bewildered by the long corridors, none of which seemed to lead her to the hub of the house. And then, all at once, she found herself at the head of the staircase, a handsome carved oak staircase leading down into a hall with a polished oak floor, where the atmosphere at that hour was twilit and cool, faintly scented with the perfume from a bowl of wax-white lilies on a black oak chest, and echoing to the light tap-tap of her heels when she crossed it on the way to the dining room.

At least she hoped it was the dining room, but there was no one about to direct her, and when she passed beneath the curtained archway she found that the room she had entered was fitted up as an extremely comfortable lounge, with windows which still stood open to the veranda where she had had tea. Standing before one of the windows, a cigarette smouldering unheeded between his fingers, was her host. He wore a white dinner-jacket which fitted his broad shoulders as if it loved them.

Elizabeth came to a halt just inside the curtained archway. Van Kane turned and looked her up and down for a moment, quite coolly. Then he said: "Dinner will be served in about a quarter of an hour. Will you have a drink?"

"No, thank you," she replied. She wore a filmy grey dress which was almost the exact colour of her eyes. Her hair formed pale golden feathers on her wide, white brow.

"No?" He cocked one of his dark eyebrows, but made no attempt to press her as he helped himself to sherry from the tray of refreshments which stood on a low polished table. Outside in the hall an unusually mellow-sounding grandfather clock, which she had subconsciously noted and admired because of its beautiful rosewood case, chimed the hour, and the sound was distilled through the quiet house like mellow music.

"So Mrs. McClegg was unable to persuade you to have something upstairs on a tray, as she phrases it, and as she seemed to consider you ought to do," he remarked, when Elizabeth had moved like an automaton in the direction of the nearest chair and seated herself. Unfortunately it was a superlatively comfortable chair which was intended to tempt its occupant to recline, and Elizabeth found it difficult to maintain a rigidly upright position, which she knew she had to do under the circumstances.

"There was no reason why anything should be brought to me upstairs," she replied, her voice as remote as her slim, straight back was almost painfully unyielding.

Nigel Van Kane's eyes glimmered with ironic humour.

"Not even an excuse you might have been looking for to avoid having dinner alone with me?"

Elizabeth's back stiffened still more.

"If I've got to recognise you as my host for the short period during which I shall be under your roof—and I hope it will be a *very* short period indeed!—then I suppose I must reconcile myself to dining alone with you sometimes; unless, of course, you would prefer it if I had my meals upstairs?" she replied, this time with lightning-like rapidity.

"Not at all," he assured her, with complete coolness and casualness. "As you are my guest—and so *long* as you are my guest!—I hope you will take advantage of all the amenities of this house, and in any case there is little point in our avoiding one another."

"But you would prefer it if we could avoid one another?" Elizabeth suggested, her hands clasping one another rather damply and tightly in her lap, while she felt as if her throat, despite strong efforts to prevent it, was working noticeably – or, at any rate, that the wild pulse-beat at the base of it, where it met her little gold cross, was noticeable.

All the humour faded out of Van Kane's face, and it grew grim all at once. She noticed, not for the first time, that he had an iron jaw, and there was something almost menacing about the way the muscles suddenly tautened in his lean cheeks, and his thin lips clamped themselves together. His voice, when he spoke, sounded exactly as if he was issuing an edict.

"There is one thing we have to get clear," he said. "You have come all the way from England to see your father, and your father has been counting the hours until you arrived. We neither of us can have any doubt that he is delighted to see you. As in the past you have done so very little for him, the opportunity which is now presented to you to make up to him in a small degree for the neglect of those years must under no circumstances be missed, and therefore you and I must forget our personal enmities and be civil to one another, at least on the surface. Is that acceptable to you?"

Elizabeth swallowed.

"My father is very ill, isn't he?"

Her host crushed out the stub of his cigarette in an ashtray and produced a flat gold case from his pocket.

"Very ill," he told her bluntly.

"What—what exactly is wrong with him?" she enquired, when she could find a strong enough voice.

The broad shoulders inside the faultless white dinner-jacket shrugged slightly, and he offered her the cigarette-case. But she shook her head dumbly.

"It was a germ he picked up years ago when he was heading that mission to Central Africa, and it has never really let him go since. And his heart is badly affected as well. In case it should strike you that the right sort of medical treatment might do a great deal for him – perhaps even cure him – you might as well know that everything possible has been done for him out here, and that he has been under the care of first class doctors. He still is under the care of a very good doctor." He looked at her without any expression in his eyes, and his cold voice continued: "There is, however, one hope. If he could recover sufficiently to stand the strain of being flown home to England, something that would yield better results might be done for him there. And it was for that reason that I encouraged him to agree to your suggestion that you should come out here and visit him—even though you would have to be a guest in my house!—because if the excitement of seeing you was not too much for him the boost to his spirits which your visit might result in might in its turn bring about an improvement in his health; sufficient, at least, to get him to England!"

Elizabeth looked down at her clasped hands. Her voice was shaky as she enquired,

"And the expense of it all? Especially the air trip? Who—who would be responsible for that?"

"I would, naturally!" came the reply, in almost deadly quiet tones, with an undercurrent of smooth, but biting sarcasm. "Who else?"

Elizabeth lifted her eyes squarely to his face, and faint banners of pink showed up clearly in her pale cheeks as she forced herself to meet the cold derisiveness of his look.

"Apparently there is no one else," she said.

He turned from her abruptly and started pacing up and down before the fireplace, a wide brick fireplace that could accommodate generous-sized logs when the evenings were cool, but was at present filled with scarlet trails of exotic-looking flowers in a gleaming copper bowl. His black brows met in a straight line of concentration above the high bridge of his nose when he burst forth at last: "We won't talk about expense, if you don't mind, in connection with your father! He and I have known one another very well, for a very long time, and anything I can do for him I shall do for him without wishing for any grateful thanks from you or from anyone! Is that clearly understood?"—with a rasping note in his voice.

"If you wish it to be understood," Elizabeth replied, in a voice that gave away nothing of what she was secretly thinking, although her fingers tightened their clasp in her lap, and the pink burned more hotly into her cheeks.

"I do," he said crisply. "And furthermore, so long as you yourself remain a guest in this house with your father, I hope that you will remember that a display of animosity is not likely to help his condition, and for that reason – however much we may mutually disapprove of one another — on the surface at least we must appear to tolerate one another. Is that also clear?"

"It would be much clearer," Elizabeth told him, her voice suddenly quivering with the indignation she found it hard to suppress, "if while we were fellow passengers in the *Star of the South* you had gone out of your way a little less to treat me as if I was an outcast, and altogether beneath your contempt! You must have known, that night when you stopped and talked to me outside the dining saloon, that I was shortly to have to accept your hospitality, and in the interests of my father and his health – which are so close to your heart!"—with a touch of sarcasm—"it might have been wiser if you had not deliberately done everything you could to antagonise me from the very beginning!"

Somewhat to her astonishment the uncompromising grimness of his expression relaxed as the result of this impulsive speech, and a gleam of humour lit his eyes. His lips also curved with amusement.

"So you do realise that I was not altogether unaware of you during the voyage?" he said. "But there were plenty of other men on board who no doubt admired you for yourself alone, and the fact that I didn't pay you any attention couldn't really have upset you!"

"It didn't!" she assured him, the words rising hotly to her lips. And she was about to add something further when a silver-toned gong boomed through the house, and he glanced at his watch and said quickly: "Dinner! You can tell me later on how much you resented my treatment of you during the voyage, but in the meantime it would be a good thing to have something to eat." He lifted his eyes from his watch and regarded her mockingly. "And after dinner I shall be spending the evening out, so you won't find it necessary to strain yourself further in an effort to convince the servants that we are friends and not enemies!"

Elizabeth said nothing, but she stood up and followed him into the dining room, which was on the other side of the hall. Amid the whirring of electric fans, and the soft-footed movements of the coloured servant who waited on them, she did her best to consume food that had no taste for her at all, although in a vague way she recognised that it was admirably served, and was probably altogether excellent if she had had the least shred of appetite, or had been less consumed by a welter of emotions inside.

She only knew that the dark red roses on the table were reflected in the polished wood of the table itself; that the lace mats were exquisite, the glass glowing and Venetian, the wine South African. Nigel Van Kane, putting himself out to be a really attentive host, explained this to her before she tasted it, and he also explained that South African wines were rapidly acquiring almost as great a popularity in the world as Spanish wines, particularly the finer types of pale sherries, such as Amontillado, Fino, and Manbanilla.

She listened to his not unattractive voice discoursing knowledgeably on the various processes which made it possible to produce wines of this quality, and the experiments that had taken place locally at a college of agriculture. And when he suggested that before her visit to Groote Kloof terminated she might be interested to observe the workings of a wine-growing farm at close quarters, she murmured politely that she would be very interested indeed, and to the ears of the listening servant there was nothing in their outward demeanour towards one another which was worthy of being commented on.

After the meal was over, Elizabeth said good night to her host, and he went out to his car that waited beneath the white-hot African stars, in a night that was noisy with the chirping of cicadas and crickets, and perfumed by the scent of hot grapes climbing the hillsides. Elizabeth heard the car start up and glide away down the drive, and she had a mental picture of the brown hands gripping the wheel, and the brown face above the white dinner-jacket, with a tiny, baffling smile on the cynical lips, and the dark eyes staring fixedly ahead.

Elizabeth wondered where he was going, and whether it was one particular friend who was drawing him forth tonight, after a day when he might have been expected to prefer to relax a little in his own comfortable home.

Then she climbed the stairs to the corridor which led to her room, turned out of it into the corridor which led to her father's room, and decided that she could not resist the urge just to look in on him. She would not disturb him if he was asleep, but if he was awake he might like to hear her say another good night to him.

Actually he was lying wide-eyed and extremely wakeful when she tapped softly on his door and entered it. His room was very similar to her own, and a light was shining dimly down on to the bed and the green counterpane and the waxen-looking face which rested on the startlingly white pillows. Elizabeth's heart turned over at the sight of that face, but she knew that the overbright eyes welcomed her. A hand was stretched out eagerly towards her, and Dr. Ransome's voice said: "How nice of you to spare me a few moments again, my dear! Mrs. McClegg said you were going early to bed, and I know you must be tired, but if you could just sit here for five minutes and let me have a good look at you! I promise I won't keep you any longer than that!"

Elizabeth swallowed something in her throat and sat down on the seat beside him. She gave him her hands and he clung on to them tightly, his eyes feverishly searching her face, taking delight in the fair and exceptionally delicate outline of it, and the way the soft hair formed those feathery fronds on her broad, intelligent brow. It was a good brow, like his own, but not so noticeably clever, and her grey eyes were very like his own, too, only large, and of course, feminine, with a poignant feminine beauty.

"Mr. Van Kane warned me that I must not excite you any further tonight," she said, softly. "He seemed to think that my arrival had excited you too much already."

"What nonsense!" Dr. Ransome exclaimed, speaking just as softly. "You can't have too much of a good thing, and you are a very good thing, Elizabeth, my dear! A sight for sore eyes! Do you know"— with a little wistful smile—"I've so often tried to picture what you were like, especially after I received one of your letters, but the only face I could conjure up was the face of the twelve-year-old Elizabeth, framed in long hair, which has always been imprinted quite ineradicably on my mind!"

Elizabeth smiled back at him.

"I've grown a bit since then."

"You have," he agreed. "You've grown into a very attractive young woman, and I'm only surprised that no one has snatched you up and married you, although it's true you're only twenty-two!" And then, continuing to gaze at her in the dim light: "No ties of that kind yet, Elizabeth? No engagement, or anything of that sort, I mean?"

Elizabeth shook her head, her eyes laughing quietly at him.

"There's been no rush to snatch me up, I do assure you, and I'm certainly not engaged – not even thinking about being engaged! Why, were you hoping to hear that you would have a son-in-law before very long?"

She spoke lightly, teasingly, but somewhat to her astonishment he answered her with perfect seriousness, following a quick shake of the head.

"Quite the contrary, my dear. I'm very much relieved that you are entirely heartwhole, and not even thinking about getting married. For one thing, I want you to stay here with me for as long as you can, without any hankerings after getting back to England, and for another ..."

"Yes?" she said, as he made no attempt to go on.

He stared upwards at the light that was swinging above them, protected by a green shade, and casting a strange green light on the ceiling. In after days Elizabeth always remembered that light, spreading outwards like a gigantic green fan towards the edges of the ceiling, and the ethereal glow it cast on the invalid's sunken cheeks.

"What do you think of Nigel?" he asked her rather abruptly. "Have you had time yet to form any serious impression of him? I know you had dinner alone together, and you must have talked ..." His voice wandered off faintly. "He's a magnificent fellow!"

Elizabeth said quietly, soothingly, because she felt that he was becoming exhausted, and she knew that she had to leave him: "I think he's very nice indeed, and he seems to be so kind to you. And now, Father, I must let you go to sleep."

He smiled up at her wearily.

"Then you do like him? Good! I didn't really think you would do anything other than like him, but I had to be sure!" All at once his eyelids drooped above his alarmingly sunken eyes, but there was a suggestion of peace about his quiet smile. "Go to bed, my dear, and have a good night's rest, and in the morning we'll have a proper natter. There's so much that I want to know."

Elizabeth bent and kissed his brow, and then she tip-toed from the room.

"Good night, Father!" she breathed, as she left him alone, and she realised that it was the first time she had said "Good night, Father!" for ten years.

# Chapter Five

The next morning Elizabeth awakened early, but she was discouraged from making an early attempt at rising by Mrs. McClegg, who brought her a breakfast tray.

"Mr. Nigel thought you'd like to have an easy morning," she observed, setting down the tray on a little table which swung across the bed, and placing an extra pillow at her back. But Elizabeth felt certain it was because he preferred to have his own breakfast alone, without an unwanted guest sharing the table with him and making it necessary for him to enter into some sort of conversation which would almost certainly prove boring when he was thinking of other things.

His stay in England had lasted for about a couple of months, but one thing she had gathered was that he was really pleased to be back, and that all his interests lay in this farm of his, which was obviously very prosperous. And she had sensed even at dinner the night before that he was keen to be back at the head of affairs, making certain that everything was running as smoothly and efficiently as he could approve.

After her breakfast she rose and dressed, and went along to her father's room, but she was told by Muemba that he was still sleeping, and so she went out to the stoep.

The beauty of the morning was something she had never really experienced before, and it gave a kind of lift to her spirits. There was a gossamer haze over everything, making even the deep blue of the sky seem as if it was viewed through a curtain of sparkling gauze. The mountains stood forth, palely violet, wrapped in a mantle of shimmering mist, and the olive trees and the fruit orchards climbing the slopes all shimmered as if they were more a figment of the imagination than an actual reality. But the sun beat down strongly, although it was still quite early in the day, and the air was hot like the pulse of summer that had come in the wake of a south-easterly wind and was prepared to settle down and stay.

Nearer at hand the garden was a riot of colour, with rambler roses climbing over arches, and a blue avenue of hydrangeas leading to a tiny, secluded corner where some of the choicest roses that bloom in English rose-gardens opened velvet petals beneath the exciting kiss of the sun, and drugged the air around them with their perfume. An attractively sited swimming pool was bounded by tall grasses and some slender, pencil-like trees and there were beds of velvet petunias, red-hot pokers, marigolds, salvias, and the absurdly English-looking hollyhocks, wherever she turned her eyes.

The quality of the lawns surprised Elizabeth, considering the unremitting attention they received at this time of the year from the sun. But they were obviously constantly watered. Every square inch of the garden was most carefully tended, as she was later to learn, and every fruit tree and vine on the estate was cosseted as if it were a human being.

She grew tired of wandering about the garden in the full blaze of the sun, and after a while she returned to the stoep and seated herself in one of the comfortable wicker chairs. Muemba brought her some coffee about eleven o'clock, and he also enquired whether she would prefer a long drink. Muemba was a magnificent specimen, so black that he appeared as if he was polished, with teeth that looked quite faultless. He had large gold rings in his ears, a little ivory tube through his nose, and he wore shorts and a tunic that were always superbly laundered.

Elizabeth had the feeling that he was amiably disposed towards her, perhaps because he was amiably disposed towards her father, and her father was an invalid.

Just before noon a blue car was driven smartly up the drive, and came to rest at the foot of the veranda steps. From it there descended a young woman who was probably a little older than Elizabeth, and who was certainly a great deal more sophisticated. She looked delightfully cool in dusty pink linen, with a wide-brimmed white hat, and under the hat as she came up the steps a pair of widely spaced violet-blue eyes fringed with the longest and blackest of eyelashes studied Elizabeth.

"You must be Elizabeth Ransome?" she said, as she held out her hand, and her smile was very noticeably friendly. "Dr. Ransome's daughter?"

Elizabeth felt almost awkward as she stood up and offered her own hand to the stranger. Compared with the diminutive size of this dainty lady in pink, the choice cut of her suit, and the perfection of every detail of her appearance, she herself was long-limbed and gauche, and her simple cotton dress, with its neat white belt that matched her white sandals, looked as if it had been picked up indiscriminately at a sale.

"I'm Carol Wainwright," the visitor told her, "and I've come to see Nigel because I've heard he's back, but it doesn't matter if he's busy, as I expect he is, because I can talk to you just as well!" She smiled with peculiar enchantment as she sank into a chair facing Elizabeth, her teeth very tiny and white and even, her skin with that curious matt surface which made Elizabeth think of a magnolia. "I've heard such a lot about you and your coming that I've been quite curious to meet you. How did you find your father?"

"I'm afraid he isn't—he isn't at all well," Elizabeth found herself replying, somewhat haltingly. "In fact—"

"In fact, he's really very ill, poor dear!" Carol Wainwright murmured sympathetically. "Yes; I know. And I know that he really is a dear, and he never grumbles or complains, or anything like that. Such a lamb-like disposition, and so unfair that he should be afflicted in this way. But he's lucky in one thing at least – he's lucky to have Nigel taking such determined care of him!"

Elizabeth felt the colour seep slowly into her cheeks, and she had the sudden uncomfortable feeling that to the shrewd eyes watching her it must look like guilty colour. She had no idea how much this lovely apparition knew of herself and the affairs of her family, but there was something about the words "determined care" which warned her that a little at least was known. Carol Wainwright was not altogether in ignorance of the situation, and for Elizabeth it was such a painful situation that she felt handicapped at the very beginning of this acquaintance.

"Mr. Van Kane is very kind," she said, "very generous to allow my father to live here with him."

"Oh, I'm sure he doesn't regard it in that light at all," Carol assured her, her violet eyes smiling in their bewitching fashion again, "and I'm sure he's just as pleased to have you here as well, because it must give your father so much pleasure." She delved into the deep pocket of her white pouch handbag and produced an elegant cigarette-case which she opened and passed to Elizabeth. "Do you think if I shouted Muemba would bring me a long, cool drink? I'm simply dying of thirst, and I'm also hoping to cadge a lunch off Nigel, because the longer I stay here the better I shall get to know you, and if you're going to stay here for any length of time we must know one another."

"It's very nice of you to say that," Elizabeth replied, in some embarrassment, for she could think of no particular reason why anyone should go out of their way to know her under the circumstances. She stood up to summon Muemba, but the servant appeared as if some unseen agency had already informed him of the arrival of the visitor, and on a tray he set down at the latter's elbow was a tall glass with ice chinking pleasantly at the bottom of it, and a large jug of lemon squash.

Carol flashed him a delighted upward glance of approval.

"How heavenly, Muemba!" she exclaimed. "Just what I needed most at exactly the right moment! How well you always look after me!"

Muemba withdrew, grinning from ear to ear, and when she had refreshed herself from the tall glass Carol explained: "It's this mounting temperature! Going up every day now until we shall soon be cooking!" She looked more curiously at Elizabeth. "Is this your first visit to Africa? And if it is, what do you think of it?"

"I haven't had very much time to make up my mind yet," Elizabeth confessed truthfully, "but my impressions are rather bewildering. The warmth is so wonderful after England in November, and then the colour is positively breathtaking. I've never seen anything like it before."

The visitor crinkled her nose and stared downwards at the ice at the bottom of her glass, shaking it.

"Oh, there's plenty of warmth – or there will be in a week or so's time! And I suppose it is a very colourful country"—looking about her rather vaguely, as if it had never really struck her that way before. "I'm your nearest neighbour – about a couple of miles away, as the crow flies, and you'll simply have to come and see me. Elandfontein is not as big as Groote Kloof, but it's as much as I can manage now that my husband is no longer with me. He was terribly keen on farming, but I'm afraid I'm not. It's the sort of thing you have to be born with an interest in."

"Yes; I suppose so," Elizabeth agreed, and with a small sensation of shock it was borne in upon her that this fascinating creature opposite her had been married, although somehow there was nothing about her that conveyed that impression. "And you have to manage alone nowadays?" she asked, more for politeness and keeping the ball of conversation rolling than for any other reason.

"Yes; since poor Bryn got himself mauled by a lion and left me a widow!"—with a little grimace.

"Oh!" Elizabeth exclaimed, thoroughly shocked. "I *am* sorry!"

Mrs. Wainwright rewarded her with a quite extraordinary little smile.

"That's very nice of you, my dear, but I'm growing accustomed to fighting my own poor little battles alone these days!" She lay back in her chair with a freshly-lighted cigarette between her flower-like lips and surveyed Elizabeth with quite embarrassing interest. "You're very English, aren't you?" she said. "With that fair hair and that astonishing complexion, exactly like peaches and cream! How on earth do you manage it? I know that I'm growing horribly sallow these days, and I shall have to try and do something about it."

Elizabeth could not conceal her astonishment this time, for a more alluringly perfect complexion than the one opposite her she had never met with in her life, and the fact that its owner deplored it on top of apparently calmly accepting the utterly gruesome horror of having her husband mauled to death by a lion was almost too much for Elizabeth.

"But to get back to what I was saying about your coming over to see me," Mrs. Wainwright said. "You'll have to come and stay with me, and that will prolong your holiday for you, and I'll comb the district for some eligible men who, even if you don't feel like taking them seriously, will at least help to make things pleasant for you. We haven't really any very interesting bachelors – apart, of course, from your present host!"—observing the glowing tip of her cigarette. "But Mark Temple can be entertaining when he chooses; he writes travel books and spends half this time trotting about the globe, and the other half with us here. At present he's here. And the Wilberforce brothers are safe but nice …"

"Oh, so you think so, do you?" a quiet, drawling voice enquired behind her, and she made a great show of being thoroughly startled as she looked over her shoulder quickly at the tall man who stood there in immaculate white drill looking down at her with an odd smile in his dark eyes.

"*Darling?*" she exclaimed, and put out a hand to him, her lustrous eyes beaming up at him. "How nice to see you again! And how nice to see you looking so one hundred per cent fit!"

"Thank you," he replied. "That, of course, is due to the voyage"—sending a direct look across at Elizabeth, who had seen him making his way quietly along the stoep from the side veranda, and was annoyed with herself because a rather breathless sensation of nervousness had attacked her, and she was afraid it was a nervousness that showed in her eyes. "It was not exactly exciting, but days at sea are always invigorating."

"I couldn't agree with you more!" Carol exclaimed, letting her fingers lie along his sleeve, and caressing it gently with the beautifully manicured tips. "But it's two years since I went to England myself, and I think it's high time I gave myself a holiday. Poor Bryn had such a lot of relatives over there that there is always someone I can stay with, and then there is his house I've got to dispose of some time or other." She sighed, and a helpless, pathetic expression crept into her face, while she seemed to cling more tightly to his sleeve. "Oh, Nigel, I have missed you, and it's really wonderful to have you back again!"

"Is it, my dear? You flatter me!" he observed, with a faintly ironical twist to his lips. He took a seat between the two of them, and once again he looked at Elizabeth. "So you two have become acquainted!" he remarked. "How long have you been chattering away like a couple of magpies before my advent? No doubt you know all each other's secrets by this time?"—very dryly.

"Don't be silly, darling!" Mrs. Wainwright exclaimed, in a sharp drawl. "Women never tell each other secrets – not the ones they consider important, anyway!" She accepted a cigarette from his case, and puffed a cloud of smoke into the air as she lay back like a voluptuous pink kitten in her chair. "But I shall carry off Miss Ransome to stay with me before she goes back to England. She'll help to relieve my loneliness, and I do often feel quite appallingly lonely," observing him under her entrancing eyelashes, which hid also the merest glimmer of a faintly seductive smile.

"And in the meantime I presume you intend to remain for lunch?" he suggested, without any sort of a smile; and then he summoned Muemba to bring drinks, and also to lay an additional place at the lunch table.

"Place already laid, baas," Muemba replied, letting his smiling dark glance rest on the visitor's slim form.

"What a gem you have in Muemba!" Carol Wainwright remarked, when the servant had withdrawn. "He really does anticipate your wishes."

"Mine? Or yours?" Nigel Van Kane inquired, his voice even more noticeably dry than before, and she had the grace to turn very, very faintly pink under his eyes.

"But, darling, I haven't seen you for such an age!" she protested. "And I know you wouldn't send me away without feeding me first!"

"How is your father?" her host asked, turning abruptly to Elizabeth. "Have you seen him this morning yet?"

"No; not yet," she admitted. "Mrs. McClegg said he was sleeping, and that he was going to have a rest today, and get up later in the afternoon if he feels like it."

"Good!" he observed shortly. "That means he's taking my advice."

During lunch Elizabeth found that it was not really necessary for her to attend very much to the conversation, for it was largely between her host and the extraordinarily attractive Mrs. Wainwright. They discussed people and places she had no knowledge of, and although they occasionally included her when mention of England cropped up, it was merely a sort of politeness on their part which she did not resent, because she preferred to sit quietly and as much unnoticed as possible while the service of the meal went forward.

The night before she had been too tired and too upset to take very much note of her surroundings, but in the full broad light of day she could not help being impressed by the dignity and the beauty of the dining room at Groote Kloof. The walls were a serene cream which went well with the magnificent wealth of oak which crossed the ceiling, and the cool, tiled floor was scattered with some very beautiful rugs. There were one or two pieces of obviously choice antique furniture, notably a carved oak dresser, and a side table which looked almost a museum piece and shone like ebony.

The few pictures on the walls were plainly just as good, and mostly Dutch. An interior by Pieter de Hooch and a placid, smiling landscape of the Holland the early settlers knew – and must often have recalled with pangs of homesickness when they were striving to eke out an existence in the strange new land that was Africa – by Van Ruysdael.

It was not a feminine room – in fact, it was intensely masculine, but the flowers on the table lent it colour, and Muemba's tall, crimson fez, which contrasted so sharply with his spotless white, provided a touch of bizarreness which, together with the white-hot sunshine that found its way into the room, created a feeling of Africa and something that was far more primitive than the house or any of its furnishings, or even its setting, so suggestive of parts of southern France.

After lunch they returned to the stoep, but Elizabeth excused herself after a while, for she had the feeling that Carol wished to be alone with her host. On the pretext of paying a visit to her father she went upstairs to her room, and she sat with a book in the opening of the tall windows which gave access to a little balcony that overlooked the back stoep, and was therefore well out of earshot of the two she had left.

Mrs. McClegg had reported, as she passed through the hall, that Dr. Ransome was proposing to join them for dinner that night, and that being the case the housekeeper recommended that he should be left alone to rest for as long as possible in order to gather together sufficient strength for the evening.

About an hour after she entered her room she heard the blue car belonging to Mrs. Wainwright move off down the drive, and then came the noise of another car starting up, and she deduced that this was the car belonging to Nigel Van Kane, and that it was bearing him on some business connected with his estate.

He did not return in time for tea, which she took alone on the front stoep, but a little before the hour when she was proposing to go and change for dinner he made his appearance in the front drive, his big dust-coloured car coming to rest at the foot of the veranda steps as it had done the afternoon before. Elizabeth looked as if she was preparing to make her escape when he descended quickly from his seat behind the wheel and signed to her to remain where she was. He shouted for Muemba, and the house-boy brought drinks, but Elizabeth would only be persuaded to accept a tall glass of iced lime, without anything stronger to give it what her host described as a "kick".

"Not even a dash of gin?" He looked at her with a rather curious gleam in his eyes, and a faint smile on his lips which she thought was a smile of faintly contemptuous amusement. "You are an abstemious young woman, aren't you? Mrs. McClegg reported that you didn't even finish the sherry I sent up to you last night! Or was that simply because I sent it?"

"Of course not." But she felt herself colouring faintly as she answered.

The look of derision in his eyes – or that was what she decided it must be – became more noticeable.

"Mrs. Wainwright asked me to say goodbye to you for her. She thinks you're very sweet, and very English! Do you find that flattering?"

"Not particularly," Elizabeth admitted truthfully, and suddenly much more calmly. "But if Mrs. Wainwright meant it to be a form of flattery, then I think it was very nice of her."

"Do you?"

"Of course."

He smiled in a way that put her teeth on edge.

"I would have said you're very English, but not susceptible to flattery, and I don't know about the sweetness. But then, of course, I hardly know you at all, do I?"

Elizabeth felt her own expression harden.

"You know me well enough—or you imagine you do!—to have decided before ever I left England that I had scarcely any virtues, and that the one or two I possibly did possess were quite negligible," she reminded him with a quiet note of acid in her voice.

"Touché" he exclaimed, and one side of his mouth lifted quizzically. "Well, we will pass over that! I was not being particularly discreet just then. But the thing I want to discuss with you – the thing I have hurried back to discuss with you, and which has worried me considerably all the afternoon, is this determination on the part of your father to have dinner with us tonight! I do feel that if possible he should be prevented from doing anything of the kind."

"Why?" All at once Elizabeth's own resentment vanished, and she looked at him anxiously. "You think that it would be too much for him?"

"Very much too much for him, I should say, considering the state of exhaustion he is in at present. Why, even dressing is an effort that taxes him nowadays, and after your arrival yesterday forty-eight hours in bed is what he needs. I've talked to him myself, but I can't shift him. Would he be likely, I wonder, to listen to you?"

"I'll go at once." She stood up, consumed by the urgent need to prevent her parent from putting an unnecessary strain upon himself by doing her what he no doubt felt was an honour that was her due, the honour of acknowledging her visit by lending her his moral support for at least one meal in the house of a stranger. But, even as she stood up, with undisguised concern on her face, Muemba appeared in the opening of the glass doors that admitted one to the lounge, and on Muemba's muscular dark arm was leaning the slight form of Dr. Ransome.

The doctor had donned evening clothes for the occasion, and although they fitted him rather loosely they made him look much more normal, and even jaunty, than he had appeared when he greeted her on her arrival. There was a rallying smile in his eyes as they rested on the two on the stoep, and he no longer looked particularly tired.

"What, not dressed yet?" he exclaimed, beaming on them both. "Run along, Elizabeth, and put on something pretty – the prettiest dress you've got in your wardrobe! I feel we must all be gay tonight! I, for one, feel gay, and I feel remarkably rested! Sensible woman, that Mrs. McClegg. She said that if I stayed in bed all day I'd be fit to join you tonight, and she was right. She was amazingly right!"

Elizabeth glanced at the face of her host, and it struck her that there was nothing very festive about his expression. It was even rather grimmer than she had seen it before. But as he felt her eyes appealing to him – and she knew inwardly that it was strange that she should be appealing to him – he met them fully for a moment, smiled in a way that transfigured his face, and would have astonished her under any other circumstances, and nodded his head.

"Yes, run along, Elizabeth," he echoed her father's words, "and let's see how enchanting you can make yourself! Give the doctor a treat – give us both a treat!"

And although he continued to gaze at her with the smile in his eyes, there was no longer any suggestion of mockery about it, and even his voice was gentle.

She left the two men on the stoep, with Muemba providing each of them with a drink, and as she went to her room to carry out their instructions she thought with a feeling of bewilderment that Nigel

Van Kane was the strangest man she had ever met, and she probably would never even begin to understand him.

But – and this was a more irrelevant thought – probably Mrs. Wainwright did!

# Chapter Six

That evening passed in a kind of haze of unreality so far as Elizabeth was concerned. She wondered what her mother and sisters would think if they could see her then, in the austere but dignified dining room with the constant whirring of the electric fans, and the white figure of Muemba passing to and from between the table and the sideboard, casting his shadow upon the cool, cream-coloured walls. Outside the light had died like a candle being abruptly extinguished, and Elizabeth had the curious feeling that night, primitive and sensuously warm, was lying crouched in the verandas, ready to rush in upon them should the mellow diffused lamp light suddenly fail.

Dr. Ransome, although he did not eat very much, talked a great deal, and his eyes dwelt fondly on the bent fair head of his daughter, where she sat facing her host at the table. The latter also surveyed her appraisingly from time to time, and whenever she lifted her eyes his seemed to be watching her, with just a hint of the old somewhat contemptuous mockery back in them.

The dress she had chosen for the evening was fine and gauzy, like the white wings of a moth, and her young, slender throat and shoulders were attractively bare. Her father had extracted a pink flower from the bowl in the centre of the table and tucked it in at the top of her dress with a gesture of sudden paternal pride.

"There!" he exclaimed, as it sent a pink flush over her cheeks. "Didn't I tell you, Nigel, that my girls were girls to be proud of? And doesn't Elizabeth prove my words?"

"She does, indeed!" his host drawled in response, and the pink flamed higher in Elizabeth's face because she was quite sure that he sounded amused.

"All this is very embarrassing, Father," she protested, anxious lest his sense of elation, coupled with the fact that they were drinking champagne – since this was something in the nature of a celebration dinner, or so Van Kane had insisted – and that he was eating practically nothing at all although obviously appreciating the quality of the dry, sparkling wine, should lead him on to further flights of unwanted flattery (unwanted because, although it was perfectly natural that he should see her through rose-tinted spectacles after so many years of not seeing her at all, she knew only too well what her host really thought of her). "And I'm quite sure Mr. Van Kane finds me, as a subject for conversation, distinctly boring."

"Not at all," the latter hastened to assure her, a little flame of humour dancing in his eyes. "On the contrary, I can sympathise very well with the feelings your father has suppressed all these years. For a daughter—even a daughter who is not always at hand!—is a daughter all the days of her life, even when, according to the old adage, she makes up her mind one day and takes a husband!"

"Ah, but Elizabeth isn't even thinking about taking a husband!" Dr. Ransome observed, almost triumphantly, turning to the suave, dark-haired figure at the head of the table. "I've already sounded her on that subject, and she isn't even considering becoming engaged. That's true, isn't it?"—turning back to Elizabeth. "That's quite true, isn't it, my dear?"

Elizabeth felt suddenly tongue-tied and acutely embarrassed. Nigel Van Kane murmured smoothly, twirling the stem of his champagne glass: "Does that mean you're entirely heartwhole, Miss Ransome? Or are you deceiving your father?"

Elizabeth felt resentment stir in her, and she stiffened.

"There would be little point in deceiving him about a thing like that, don't you agree?" she suggested, very quietly.

The dark, entertained eyes confused her.

"It all depends how very recent the affair was, and how much you were afraid the doctor here might not approve," he replied, in those annoying smooth tones. "For instance, you could have lost your heart on the boat coming out here, couldn't you? It has been done before, you know – by just as resistant types as yourself! Perhaps even more resistant! The general effect of moonlight, and warm seas, and being cut off from the prosaic everyday world does do these things. That's part of the attraction of a voyage."

Elizabeth stared down at the portion of feathery-light soufflé that had just been placed in front of her by Muemba, and she bit her lip.

"Is it?" she said, beginning to attack the soufflé.

"You should know!" he told her annoyingly.

"But I've only made one voyage, and you've probably made many, so your information on that head must be considerably greater than mine," Elizabeth flashed at him, with a deceptively demure upward glance.

Her host smiled suddenly, revealing his beautifully hard white teeth.

"Well, you could of course have something there," he agreed.

Dr. Ransome looked faintly perplexed by this interchange, and he also began to frown.

"When Elizabeth does lose her heart I hope it will not be as the result of a little moonlight, or anything evanescent like that," he remarked quietly. "Marriage is not founded on moonbeams, and shipboard affairs are usually highly unsatisfactory. When you do marry, Elizabeth"—looking at her gravely—"pick someone you can bear to live with in the most unromantic surroundings, should things work out like that, and for whom you would be prepared to make sacrifices, and devote the whole of your life to, whatever the circumstances, and however great the sacrifice. Otherwise, do not marry at all"—with a shadowed look on his face. "That is my advice to you."

"So there you are!" Van Kane exclaimed. "And beware of African moonlight, for it can be dangerous!"

Elizabeth was quite sure now that he was openly and deliberately mocking her, and she was glad when the dinner was ended and they withdrew to the front stoep, where Muemba served them with coffee. Her father, although he was beginning to look more tired now, and showing signs of nervous strain, declined to be persuaded to return to his own room, and as he stretched himself in his long wicker chair with a light rug over his knees, despite the warmth of the night, he declared that he was very comfortable, and almost completely happy.

"This is something I have looked forward to for a long time," he announced simply, with a devoted look at Elizabeth, lying gracefully in her own cane chair, and more than ever like an insubstantial moth in the gloom. "To have you here, knowing that you're going to stay with me for some time, and that you like being here!" He bent towards her and patted her hand, where it rested on the arm of her chair. "And having Nigel, too! Nigel"—with an affectionate glance— "is never anything but good to me!"

Elizabeth felt something like a lump rise up in her throat, but she swallowed it determinedly. She smiled tenderly at the fragile form of her father, regretting the years that they had spent apart, when she might have done so much for him. She even felt that for his sake she must endeavour to combat her instinctive dislike for, and mistrust of, their mutual host, Nigel Van Kane.

She refilled the coffee cups, and tucked the rug in carefully over her father's knees. She felt that she wanted to do a great many things for him, but there was little enough she could do.

The host began to talk more pleasantly on subjects that were less likely to make her feel self-conscious, or put her on the defensive, and these subjects included Africa, and the many and varied aspects of African life. As he put it, the vast continent was still a map that was only half unfurled, and much of it still lay well below the level of occidental thought and reasoning. It was too vast a subject to be dismissed by anyone who was not prepared to probe and think deeply – and at least to attempt to unfurl a little more of the map.

Africa ...! As she lay there in the darkness, with only the light from the lounge windows behind her streaming out across the stoep and just penetrating the inky fringes of the lawns, Elizabeth thought that the heavy, scented silence, broken only by the calm and unhurried and quite pleasing voice of Van Kane – when he was not being deliberately provocative – ought suddenly to be shattered by the low, ominous roar of a lion, or some other untameable creature of the wilds, to convince her of the reality of her being there.

She realised all at once that her host had stopped talking, that her father had stopped answering and appeared to have fallen asleep, and that he looked very peaceful with his grey head resting against the cushions behind him.

Van Kane was smoking a cigarette, and staring reflectively into the shadows. A light like a lantern climbing into the immense void that was the sky was slowly revealing the tops of the trees, and the shadows beyond the lawn looked a little less menacing. The lantern-light spread in all directions until even the paths were discernible, and the whole of the garden was bathed in a flood of silver light.

"What about stretching your legs?" Van Kane enquired, and Elizabeth looked across at him as if startled by the suggestion.

But, nevertheless, she stood up at once, and she felt rather than saw him smile as he came up behind her and took her arm and guided her down the steps and on to the crisp surface of the lawn.

"You think our nights are a bit sinister, don't you?" he said, while the smile still clung about his mouth.

Elizabeth did not answer, but her willingness to permit him to retain possession of her arm answered for her, and she did feel absurdly unsure of herself as they went forward along the narrow paths, beneath the riotous masses of Dorothy Perkins, and the enormous African stars, the splendour of which was dimmed slightly now by the rising of the moon.

Van Kane's hold of her bare arm was firm and comforting, and his fingers, although they grasped her securely, made no indentations into her flesh. They were warm, virile fingers that prevented her feeling panic-stricken when something seemed to move in the path ahead of them – although she realised that it was probably only a trick of her imagination – and the thought of snakes occurred to her, and she wondered what it would be like to set her foot on one.

Were there snakes in this vine-clad region? Or did they only belong to the more primitive corners of the continent, like the lions and the leopards who were nowadays almost only found in national parks and game preserves?

Elizabeth felt she would almost sooner come face to face with a lion than set her foot on a snake. And when her thin evening slipper did come down on something that seemed to wriggle and writhe beneath it and then escape she was so profoundly horror-stricken that for one moment she could not even cry out, and then she turned and clutched at the man beside her, holding him so tightly and with such trembling fingers that he exclaimed softly, in amazement:

"And now what?"

Elizabeth leant against him abashed by what she had done, but still possessed by her fear. The horrible moment when whatever it was that had wriggled and writhed beneath her foot had finally made its escape was still with her, and there was a note like hysteria in her voice as she cried out: "It was a snake! Or—or it felt like a snake! And I trod on it …!"

She shuddered, clinging to him.

He produced a torch from his pocket and shone its broad beam across the path, covering the area they had so recently traversed. A bare yard from where they stood a piece of innocent-looking root, about an inch thick, was lying, and there were various fibres attaching to it which proved beyond doubt, and at a single glance, that it was nothing more than a root. Elizabeth gazed at it at first unbelievingly, and then with a kind of hot blush rising up all over her body as her host's voice informed her, with undisguised amusement in it: "There's your snake! Probably the most harmless one I've ever encountered!"

He freed himself from her still somewhat convulsively clutching fingers and went back along the path and picked up the piece of root. He held it out to her to feel, but Elizabeth's eyes were miserable with embarrassment, and she put her hands behind her back and stood awkwardly before him, declining to so much as touch it.

"What an idiot you must think me!" Her eyes appealed to him, and even the rounded tip of her chin was rosy in the remorseless light of the torch. She was biting her lower lip hard, as if to steady it.

"As a matter of fact, I don't think anything of the kind," he answered, and although she was sure he was laughing at her inwardly, there was a new and quite surprising note of gentleness in his voice. He put an arm about her and held her quite strongly against his side while he added, rather more softly: "But I'll tell you what I do think, shall I? I think rather more than you've felt able to cope with has happened to you over the past two days, and it's shaken you a bit. And I also think you're very young – and not a bit tough! Not really!"

He looked down at the top of her head with a smile in his eyes which she did not see, and then he suggested: "Shall we go back to the house, and postpone our moonlit exploration of the grounds until another night?"

Elizabeth nodded, silently. She felt stupid, and so ashamed of herself and the way in which she had laid hands upon him, that it rendered her unable to speak without betraying the fact that her voice would have a break in the middle. And she was quite sure that in addition to despising her for quite another reason he would now be inclined to regard her as contemptibly timid as well, and altogether a poor thing – just as poor a thing as he had imagined she would be before ever she arrived!

But he didn't sound as if he held her in very much contempt as he remarked soothingly on the way back to the house: "If I were you, I'd go to bed early again tonight, and we'll pack that father of yours off to bed, too. I do realise that seeing him as he is has shocked you considerably, but he may perk up enormously now that you've arrived. He's certainly been better this evening than I've known him to be for a long time, and I believe he's fully prepared to enjoy your visit. You may act upon him like a tonic. But we mustn't let him stay up and overdo things tonight. Just speak to him firmly, and I'll back you up."

Elizabeth nodded again. As they crossed the lawn towards the front veranda steps they could see Muemba near the chair in which Dr. Ransome had fallen asleep, obviously taking it upon himself to wake him.

Muemba seemed to be bending concernedly over the doctor – probably thinking that he had already been up far too long – and in the golden light which streamed from the wide windows behind him his tall fez and snowy garments showed up clearly.

At the sound of their footsteps ascending the steps Muemba turned, and in his polished dark face the whites of his eyes showed up almost alarmingly, but there was no flash of white teeth as his lips parted in their customary wide grin. He did not grin at all. And he spoke rapidly.

"Baas sleep too long, baas! Baas not waking easily …!"

Nigel Van Kane went forward and stood beside his old friend's chair. He bent over him, even as Muemba had done, and placed his hand very gently on his shoulder.

"Wake up, Ransome! It's time for bed, and Muemba's getting anxious."

Then he bent lower, peered keenly in the diffused golden light, saw that the doctor was very fast asleep indeed, with an unusually peaceful expression on his face, and straightened abruptly. For a moment he stood absolutely still, and then he turned as Elizabeth touched his arm.

"There's nothing wrong, is there? He's quite all right—?"

Her voice was uncertain, frightened. Somehow she knew that Dr. Ransome was not all right.

And then a hand caught hold of hers and gripped it tightly, so tightly that she actually winced. A pair of dark eyes with strange little golden lights in them that reminded her of lights floating in a sea of darkness looked down at her, and from an immeasurable distance, as it seemed to her then, her host's voice spoke to her – only it didn't sound like her host's voice at all, not even the voice that had addressed her quite gently only a bare few minutes before.

"Yes; he's all right," he answered. "*He's* all right! But you've got to prove that you really are his daughter, and try and get it into your head that this was the best way out for him – the way he would have chosen! And he was happy tonight!"

# Chapter Seven

It was the week before Christmas, and with the temperature steadily rising Cape Town prepared for Christmas festivities and lay bathed in summer sunlight.

To Elizabeth there was something quite incongruous about little dabs of cotton-wool and scarlet-robed figures of Santa Claus driving sprightly teams of reindeer behind the plate-glass windows of Adderley Street. And Christmas shoppers loaded with parcels and wearing the flimsiest of cotton dresses, and even sun-suits, struck her as particularly odd.

She was on a shopping expedition herself with Carol Wainwright, with whom she had been staying for several weeks, and since Carol was a South African and had only once in her life spent a winter in a northern latitude, the conditions that prevailed at the Cape in December were to her completely normal. And although she sometimes complained of the heat she never really looked as if it affected her. She was always spruce and cool — at any time to look at – and delectably turned out, and since a large part of her wardrobe came to her direct from Paris it was not surprising that wherever she appeared in public men's heads were turned to gaze at her.

Today she was rather more enchanting than usual in a flowered dress and an enormous shady hat, and after lunch in the cool dining room of one of the bigger hotels she announced to Elizabeth that Mark Temple had been persuaded to spend Christmas with them, and that she was hopeful that quite a few people would be joining them for Christmas Day dinner. And on Boxing Day she was throwing something in the nature of a real party.

"You'll like Mark," she said, as Elizabeth made polite responses. "He's been to China or somewhere during the past few months, but when we do see him again after one of his disappearances it's always almost as good as a tonic. He's not strictly conventional, sometimes a bit cynical, but he's refreshing. And Nigel *may* honour us with a visit over the holiday period!"

Elizabeth was quite certain that as this last piece of information was offered to her Mrs. Wainwright was watching her rather carefully beneath the deep brim of her hat in order to observe her reactions. But Elizabeth stared hard at her plate and tried to prevent any sort of noticeable expression from appearing in her face, for although on the surface they were the best of friends, and Elizabeth was really grateful to her attractive hostess for keeping her so long, there were moments when she was by no means altogether certain of her, and when she even asked herself how much longer she could endure to remain a guest beneath her roof.

It was true that it was Nigel who had insisted on her accepting Mrs. Wainwright's invitation, pointing out to her that there was no other course open to her, now her father was no longer alive, unless she returned home to England, for the Van Kane household was a bachelor one. But for close upon a fortnight now she had been making up her mind to break it to her hostess that she was determined to return to England quite soon.

For it was one thing to accept hospitality, and it was another to go on accepting it. And where Nigel Van Kane himself was concerned there was always an element of—something she could never be quite clear about, but which puzzled and disturbed her, and which sprang into the atmosphere between them whenever his name was mentioned, or accidentally found its way into the conversation.

Carol Wainwright had a way of regarding her, Elizabeth, with a kind of dubious amusement in her eyes – sometimes a curious, speculative amusement, which Elizabeth always felt was not particularly friendly, either – when the subject of him arose.

"Of course," Carol had said once, shortly after Dr. Ransome's sudden death, "I know he was a very good friend to your father, and I believe for some reason there was a kind of bond between them, but for that reason alone you will not go on keeping in touch with him, will you? *Or* allow him to interfere in your affairs! Oh, I know he's inclined to regard you as rather helpless"—smiling in a way that made Elizabeth feel that she really ought to do something about it, and if she was helpless it was the kind of helplessness that could, and did, evoke amusement sometimes—"but he's the sort of man who often troubles himself over the affairs of other people whom he considers to be weaker and less able to cope with things than himself, and if he displays interest then it shouldn't be allowed to affect one's judgment, or assume any sort of special significance. Not, I'm sure"—with a more conciliatory and altogether engaging smile—"that a girl of your age would ever feel interest in a man who was very nearly fifteen years older than herself, so I don't think I need bother to warn you."

But Elizabeth realised that she was warning her just the same, and she was well aware of the reason why Carol considered a warning necessary.

For after the death of her father, occurring as it did at a time when she had had no opportunity to recover from the shock of discovering that he was ill, Elizabeth had, she knew, gone more or less to pieces. For days she had been so stunned by the unexpectedness of events that but for the presence of one man she might have been more seriously affected by the harsh reality which she had been so ruthlessly brought up against than she had been. But Nigel Van Kane, whom she had disliked so violently when she arrived at Groote Kloof, had been like a lifeline flung to her in the first shock of bereavement. She would never have believed that it was on his strangely rock-like strength, the human consolation in his voice, and the comfort of his strongly grasping hands that she would depend in those first numb hours of bewilderment when tragedy crossed her path for the first time; but it had been so.

The grief she felt at her father's death was not the grief she might have felt had they never been separated from one another; the remorse she experienced because she had left her coming to join him so late was the thing which racked her, and which tortured her every time she thought about it.

For forty-eight hours he had been happy to know that she was with him, but what was forty-eight hours when he had had so many years of being cut off altogether from his family?

Where would he have been without Nigel Van Kane?

He had never had a son, but Nigel had been better than a son to him for years!

Elizabeth felt that nothing could be said to justify her own inertia and neglect of her father's well-being. Her mother and sisters just did not enter into it, but she had corresponded with him for years, and she should have been able to read between the uninformative lines of his letters and realise that all was not well with him. His very silence on the subject of himself and his health should have struck her as odd, if nothing else.

But the fact that he had provided adequately for all four members of his family and left himself so bereft of this world's goods that he had had to become dependent on the generosity of a good friend was the thing which had shocked her most.

In the midst of her self-condemnation she recognised numbly that now was the time for Nigel to turn and rend her. That he did not do so amazed her, and that instead of doing so he provided her with moral support, saw to her physical well-being, and concerned himself with lessening and mitigating her period of shock, and even interested himself in her future welfare, was something she could barely understand.

His home became a refuge to her at that time—even as it had to her father!—and Mrs. McClegg, who had nursed him as a baby, fussed round her in a way that surely indicated that in addition to her own natural kindness of heart she had received special instructions to do all that she could to make things less trying for Elizabeth. And when, at the end of a week, Mrs. Wainwright had arrived to take her back to her own house – she would have arrived earlier, she said, but for the fact that she had been visiting in Durban, and had only heard of the tragedy a few hours before – Elizabeth herself was amazed at the strong disinclination she felt to become a guest at Elandfontein and leave what she now regarded the sanctuary of Groote Kloof.

Groote Kloof had not welcomed her on arrival, but she was so keenly sorry to go away from it that she could not altogether understand her own reluctance. She looked wistfully at the stoep where her father had sat, and where he had died, on the morning she left, and as she was carried smoothly away down the short drive in Mrs. Wainwright's smart blue car she wondered whether she would ever see the place again, and was quite sure she would not.

Nigel Van Kane, as she recognised inwardly, must have been both relieved and glad to hand her over to the temporary care of someone else, but his consideration, for her lasted until the moment when he took his farewell of her.

His eyes smiled down at her encouragingly – extraordinary, she thought now, that she should have ever thought that they were hard eyes, and if they mocked sometimes still it was a friendly mockery. He took both her hands and retained them within his own for several seconds, while Carol Wainwright stood and regarded them both with a fixed, cool smile on her lips and an enigmatic gleam in her eyes, and Muemba stacked the luggage in the car.

"Now don't think you've got to run away back to England because you've no longer any sort of a tie in this country," he said. "You spent a lot of money on your passage out here, and you must reap some sort of a benefit. Carol is delighted to have you stay with her, and you can stay with her as long as you please – isn't that right, Carol?"

"Of course, darling," But Carol was tapping the ground impatiently with the toe of her white-shod foot. "Elizabeth knows all that, and she also knows that I plan to give her a very good time and do all that I can to help her forget the horrid time she has had here. Poor lamb! She wants some nice, bright young men friends, and a party or two to set her on her feet! And that's what I'm prescribing for her."

"Well, I'd keep the men friends down to a reasonable number"—the dark eyes with the golden lights in them were smiling pleasantly, but apart from the smile they were as enigmatic as her own as they gazed back into Mrs. Wainwright's—"otherwise you'll have Elizabeth confused! The Wilberforce lads might measure up to her very well, as they're about her own age; but I wouldn't recommend the more sophisticated types – at any rate, not yet!"

"That's what you think!" She flickered her eyelashes at him. "But Elizabeth and I probably think quite otherwise!"

With an alluring smile she climbed into the seat behind the wheel of the car, and as they moved off Elizabeth felt suddenly a little sick inside. She was not looking forward to anything in the nature of a whirl of gaiety, but she did know a sudden almost overpowering desire to leap out of the car while it was still moving and run back to the man who was standing very tall and upright at the foot of the veranda steps, watching their departure with a strangely inscrutable expression on his face.

He had been a pillar of strength to her over the past few days, and without him she was going to feel oddly at a loss. But she had got to get used to being at a loss.

And even as they sped down the drive Carol, with her slim hands grasping the wheel, and the smile still clinging to her lips, observed: "And I meant what I said just now, Elizabeth, my dear! You *are* going to have a good time, and once out of a strictly bachelor household you'll be able to relax, and you won't have that nasty, niggly uneasiness at the back of your mind because, however broad-minded one might be and however much Nigel is revered in this part of the world for his moral integrity and so forth, it isn't *quite* the right thing to go on living beneath the roof of a bachelor while he happens to be living there, too!" She swung the car out between the gates and on to the reasonably good strip of road, put her foot on the accelerator and added: "And there are always people who talk! And you can't stop them talking, especially when a young and pretty girl is in the picture, *and* an attractive man!"

Elizabeth said nothing, but she felt that her prospective hostess had delivered herself of an opinion that she was determined to air before she started out. Having done so, she could become all sweetness and gracious hospitality, and the little sideways smile she directed at Elizabeth was intended to rob her words of any sting they might possess, or anything that could make her uncomfortable.

And in the following weeks she certainly went out of her way to fulfil the promises she had made to Elizabeth and Nigel. She did ask quite a lot of people to Elandfontein to meet Elizabeth, and on most days there was someone with whom Elizabeth could play tennis, or dance in the evenings, if she wished to. The Wilberforce brothers – of whom her recent host had approved — were muscular, wholesome, and reasonably attractive youths, running a joint farm, and as that farm was not far away they found plenty of excuses for looking in on Mrs. Wainwright.

Nigel Van Kane alone did not avail himself of Carol's notoriously generous hospitality to any very great extent, at any rate during the early weeks of Elizabeth's stay with her. He dined with them once, and he lunched with them once, but on each occasion he left very soon after the meal, and Elizabeth had no opportunity to talk to him, On the second occasion she had the feeling that he wished to talk to her, and his eyes dwelt on her consideringly while they were at the table; but so soon as they left the table Carol seized his arm and led him off to a corner of her wide veranda for what she termed "a cosy little chat," and one of the other guests appropriated Elizabeth and persuaded her to play tennis.

When they all foregathered for tea Nigel had already departed, and Carol, with a gay look across at Elizabeth, informed her that she had been entrusted with his farewells to her, and that he was sorry he had had to leave without saying them to her personally.

Elizabeth, although she realised that there was no reason at all why he should have delayed his departure until she had won free from the tennis-court, was yet conscious of a quick stab of disappointment because he had not said goodbye to her himself. And it was a disappointment which must have showed in her face, for she caught Mrs. Wainwright looking at her rather quizzically.

And now she learned that he *might* honour them with a visit over the Christmas holiday.

On the way back to Elandfontein Carol seemed in a particularly blithe and amiable mood, and she drove her blue car in a slightly reckless manner, as she always did when she was at the top of her form.

At the foot of the veranda steps when they reached the house another car was standing, and it was not nearly such an up-to-date and well-cared-for specimen as the one which came to rest behind it. In fact, it had every appearance of being of ancient vintage, and it also bore the marks of much usage. But Carol, when she caught sight of it, uttered a little exclamation which sounded like genuine pleasure, and she sprang nimbly out of her own car and up the steps of the veranda and gave her hands to the man who stood somewhat inelegantly leaning against one of the supporting posts, and obviously waiting to be noticed.

He was not particularly tall, and the first thing Elizabeth noticed about him was that he had flaming red hair, and a skin that was the colour of well-seasoned mahogany. He wore khaki shorts, and a khaki shirt open at the throat, and there was a pipe gripped between his teeth, which he removed as Mrs. Wainwright caught at him almost convulsively.

"Mark!" she exclaimed. "Oh, Mark, you villain! And I didn't expect you for another few days at least!"

White teeth flashed in the sunshine as Mark Temple smiled lazily. He had greenish-hazel eyes which stared coolly downwards at Elizabeth.

"Then think what a pleasant surprise I've let you in for," he said. He was still staring at Elizabeth. "Aren't you going to introduce me to your friend? I'm quite certain I've never met her before, otherwise the meeting would have impressed itself upon me." Elizabeth had collected the parcels and was coming slowly up the steps. She was wearing her lime-green linen, and she looked very young and cool and fresh, and her expression was attractively shy. Mark Temple removed the parcels from her arms and set them down on a table, and then he possessed himself of one of her hands and held it firmly for much longer than was strictly conventional, while with the same absence of conventionality he made an embarrassingly cool survey of her face.

Carol introduced them. Elizabeth managed to regain possession of her hand, and her hostess smiled in an amused fashion because her young visitor was obviously not accustomed to anyone as deliberate as Mark Temple.

"It's all right, my dear," she said. "Mark is a connoisseur of pretty faces, and yours obviously intrigues him. But I warn you that he's not to be trusted, and anything he may say to you when he gets you alone will have to be dismissed as mere flattery, because he says the same thing to all of us."

But, nevertheless, she was quite plainly delighted because he had arrived considerably in advance of the date she expected him, and when he airily said that he imagined the room he usually occupied was ready for him, she assured him that it was. But for Elizabeth's benefit she added the information that during her husband's lifetime Mark had looked upon that room as almost belonging to him, and that they had known one another for years.

"So we're not as unconventional as we may seem," she said.

When Elizabeth went away to change for dinner she left the two of them alone in the veranda, and while she was dressing she could hear their voices, at first exchanging light badinage, finally dropping away to lower tones which seemed to indicate that their conversation had taken on a more serious or personal note. When she returned to the veranda they were still lying in long cane chairs, with glasses of sherry at their elbows, and Mrs. Wainwright looked like a contented kitten in her flowered dress, with her dark head — it was so sleek and dark that the close-cropped hair looked like a black satin cap, with one or two smooth curls lying softly on the wide white brow in front – nestled amongst the brightly coloured cushions behind her.

They both looked upwards at Elizabeth, rather uncertain of herself and her welcome just then in a demure blue chiffon dress that was quite unsophisticated and made her eyes look rather more blue than grey, and very wide and not too happy under their feathery gold brows. Mrs. Wainwright yawned, just like a sleepy kitten, and she seemed to study Elizabeth for a moment with interest before she announced that she supposed she really would have to go and change.

"Why bother?" Mark Temple enquired, lying back in his own chair and looking thoroughly comfortable, and loath to disturb himself. "We waste such a lot of time troubling about appearances, and in any case I must say you look altogether enchanting as you are"—turning his eyes slowly in the direction of his hostess. "As," he added, with lazy distinctness, "you always do, anyway – to me, at least!"

Carol Wainwright, who had risen with one graceful movement from her chair, looked down at him for a moment with the same sort of contemplative consideration in her look as had dwelt in her eyes when she studied Elizabeth, and then she thanked him, with a faintly mocking smile.

"That," she said, turning to Elizabeth, "is the sort of thing to expect from Mark – and the thing I warned you about! Flattery!"

After which she left them alone on the veranda, and he grinned at Elizabeth, and the latter had to admit it was an engaging grin.

"Come and have a drink," he invited. "And come and tell me all about yourself and how long you propose to remain in Africa."

# Chapter Eight

It was on Christmas Eve that Nigel Van Kane made his appearance at Elandfontein, his first appearance for close upon three weeks.

There had been one or two people for lunch — including, of course Mark Temple – and they were all sitting about in somnolent attitudes in comfortable wicker chairs on the front veranda when he drove his powerful dust-coloured car up to the front of the steps. Carol stood up at once to greet him. She looked elegant and in her element as an admittedly charming hostess, but her eyes reproached him.

"Why on earth couldn't you make the effort to get here for lunch?" she chided him. "I expected you – we all expected you!"

"Did you?" His eyes were cool and remote. "I was busy," he explained. "Very busy!" He looked at the cluster of people in front of him, and he seemed to be searching for one who was not there. "Hallo, Mark!" he said. "So you're back again!" And then, quietly: "Where's Elizabeth?"

Carol smiled rather oddly.

"She's in her room, writing letters, I believe. I simply can't get it into her head that one doesn't do that sort of thing in the heat of the day. But she's had some presents from England, and she's acknowledging them at once. Elizabeth is extraordinarily meticulous in some ways."

"A good thing to be," Mark Temple observed, but Nigel said nothing, only gave a hitch to his immaculate trousers and sat down in a vacant chair.

After a time one or two of the guests departed in their cars of mixed vintage, and those that were left decided to play tennis. Carol, as the hostess, had to help make up a four, but the latest arrival declined to give up his chair in the veranda.

"I feel idle," he told her, smiling at her in a lazy fashion, "and I shall sit here and become contemplative. Besides, I want to talk to Elizabeth when she makes her appearance."

"Do you want me to give her a call?" But although her smooth, pale face gave away little of what she was actually thinking, and it was more like a beautiful, provocative mask than anything else, he had the feeling that she was not altogether pleased with him just then, and that she had no intention of calling Elizabeth. She was merely delaying the moment before she joined the others on the court. "Will you be staying for dinner tonight?"

"I'm not quite sure." The little gold lights in his eyes confounded her, and she bit her scarlet lower lip. "It all depends."

"On what?"

"On one thing in particular, and also whether or not you'd like me to stay. You haven't issued a formal invitation, you know!"

Carol's eyes revealed sudden frustration.

"I invited you to lunch, but you didn't arrive in time for it, did you? And if I ask you to stay for dinner tonight you're just as likely to think up an excuse. You're rather good at thinking up excuses these days, aren't you, Nigel?"

"Am I?" But the little annoying smile refused to be banished from his eyes.

"You know you are!" Her teeth dug harder into the soft flesh of her lower lip. "And I think it's rather beastly of you!"

His eyes went suddenly completely inscrutable.

"I'm sorry, my dear, but it's your imagination that is entirely at fault. You allow it to work overtime. But if you really are prepared to put up with me for dinner tonight—and Mark is prepared to put up with me as well!—then I'll be very happy to stay. Does that satisfy you?"

His hostess looked as if she wished she could penetrate that uninformative facade that was the lean, dark mask of his face, but past experience had taught her that that was never possible when Nigel Van Kane decided that no one should get past the barrier he put up. And she sighed suddenly.

"It's nothing to do with Mark. You know that. And of course I'd like you to stay."

"Good!" he exclaimed softly. "Then I'll stay."

As she was about to turn away and leave him she recollected that he had said something else rather strange, and she turned back abruptly and demanded to know what he had meant when he said that his remaining depended "on one thing in particular." But to her increased annoyance he merely smiled and shook his head.

"Shall we say that it depended on how much you wanted me to stay, and leave it at that?" he suggested.

Mrs. Wainwright looked suddenly almost furious.

"Sometimes I think you're impossible!" she declared, and hurried away down the path through the golden warmth which flooded the garden in the direction of the tennis-court, her thickly pleated cream skirt swaying indignantly as she moved.

For perhaps ten minutes he lay quietly in his chair, smoking a cigarette and surveying the green lawn in front of him under drooping eyelids. The lawn was perhaps not as well tended as his own, but it was restful to the eye, and it was bordered by beds of brilliant flowers. Beyond it there was a white arch – startlingly white in the sunshine – with a slave bell hanging beneath it, and on the other side of the arch were grouped the storehouses, the barns and the stables which made up the farm buildings, all silhouetted against the brazen blue of the sky.

Stretching himself luxuriously in his chair, Nigel Van Kane looked upwards at that blue sky, and then he closed his eyes and appeared to be thinking of drifting into tranquil sleep where he sat. But a sudden slight movement behind him caused him to open his eyes again quickly, and he looked round as Elizabeth made her appearance, hesitatingly, in the opening of the lounge windows behind him.

Elizabeth had known for the past half-hour that he was there — in fact, she had heard his car drive up to the front of the house. But a curiously paralysing attack of combined nervousness and shyness had prevented her from doing the natural thing and going downstairs to meet him while the others were all there. Her letters were finished, and she had no longer any excuse for lingering in the little room which was not nearly so attractively furnished, or as comfortable in a practical way, as the one she had occupied at Groote Kloof, but for some reason she couldn't find the strength of will to force her to go out to the veranda.

Not until the sudden, deceptive silence convinced her that the veranda was at last deserted, and everyone either playing tennis or gone to their own homes. And then, after a hasty examination of herself in her dressing-table mirror, she had stolen down the bare oak stairs to the whitewashed lounge, which her hostess had made gay with somewhat bizarre furnishings, and parted the glass doors to the veranda. And at sight of the long-limbed figure in the rattan chair she felt all her pulses give a sudden, wild leap, and she stood absolutely still.

"Hallo, Elizabeth!" Nigel Van Kane's voice was very quiet. He stood up and moved slowly towards her, smiling slightly and holding out his hand. "How are you?"

Elizabeth was wearing a blue-and-white linen dress, white sandals and a white belt, and she looked large-eyed and somehow defenceless. But as she gave him her hand and felt his cool, firm fingers take hold of it and retain it in his clasp he could not doubt that, behind her obvious shyness, she was quite glad to see him.

"I understand you've received a shower of Christmas presents and have been dealing with your correspondence," the man said, as she drew forward one of the empty chairs for her. He smiled at her more warmly. "Shall I wish you a merry Christmas, Elizabeth, or doesn't it seem like Christmas out here to you?"

"It doesn't," Elizabeth admitted truthfully. She was sitting very upright and gazing at him, thinking how good it was to see him after all this time, and wondering why it was that in the early days of their acquaintance — and particularly when they were fellow passengers in the *Star of the South* – she had formed the opinion that he was not at all handsome, although even then she had recognised that there was *something* about him that would always single him out from amongst other men. Now she was prepared to concede that he was almost strikingly good-looking with that sleek, dark head, that ruthless line of bronzed chin and jaw, those very thick eyelashes that could conceal, when he wished them to do so, the little glints in his dark eyes, and his strong mouth and faultless white teeth.

"Does that mean you're feeling homesick?" he asked, watching her with sudden keenness.

"Oh, no!" Elizabeth hastened to reassure him. As a matter of fact, she could not even explain to herself what her feelings were just then, and not only about the festival of the Birth of Christ in a land that was altogether new to her. She knew that her people at home – her mother and her sisters – would be making preparations for the season in the way that they had always done, and to which she was accustomed; but she was not conscious of any particular yearning to be with them. Their holly and their mistletoe, the trappings of their Christmas tree, the orgy of present-giving they would indulge in seemed hardly real to her in this bright, sunny land. If she was not entirely happy, it was partly because of her father's death and partly because she still did not feel wholly welcome in the farmhouse to which Bryn Wainwright had brought his lovely bride five years before, and where she was now both mistress and master and a widow at twenty-six.

Sometimes Elizabeth even had the feeling that her hostess was merely suffering her presence in the house for some purpose of her own which was impossible to guess at, and that there were occasions when the inexperience and slight rawness of the English girl irked her more than she was able to show. At others, Carol could be completely charming, and was ready to assure Elizabeth that she could stay with her as long as she liked, and that she loved having her. She always hinting that it would be a good thing if she married one of the local young men who had shown signs of admiring her, but Elizabeth was well aware that her heart was not in the least likely to be involved where any of those young men were concerned. And she resented having young men more or less thrust at her in the playful way Carol had of doing these things, and being expected to fall in with someone's wishes and marry because it was a good idea.

When, and if, she ever did marry, it would not be because it was "a good idea" – or so she told herself. Marriage had to be for something far, far more important than that, as her father, on that last night of his life, had tried to impress on her, and on Nigel Van Kane.

"I believe you are homesick all the same," Van Kane said suddenly, after a prolonged period of studying her face. For Elizabeth's face was both fair and revealing, and it was thinner than when he had seen it last. Her eyes had brightened, somewhat to his astonishment, when she first had come face to face with him on the veranda, but now that she was sitting opposite to him with her hands clasped rather tightly together in her lap – an attitude which betrayed nervous tension – he could see that there was a certain faintly wistful droop to her lips, and her eyes were clouded. She was not happy – she was certainly not at her ease, and he gathered the fact that she seldom was at her ease in this house. She was trying all the time to be the ideal guest and fit in with her hostess's ways, but they were not her ways.

"Do you still think very much about your father?" he asked rather abruptly.

"Naturally, I haven't forgotten him," she answered quietly. "And it's not many weeks since he died, is it?"

"No."

Suddenly he stood up and put a hand beneath her elbow to assist her to rise also.

"We're liable to be interrupted here," he said, "and I want to talk to you. Come with me and we'll find a spot where we can count upon being undisturbed for a short while at least."

# Chapter Nine

The spot, when they found it, was cool and shut in by trees, and there was a blaze of cannas in front of their eyes when they sat down in a couple of chairs which someone with an eye to solitude and the desirability of maintaining that solitude had placed there. The chairs were rather close together, and Elizabeth could feel the man's thin sleeve brushing her arm when they were both seated.

He offered her a cigarette and lighted it for her, and then there was a somewhat protracted moment of silence. At last: "What are you going to do when you leave Carol?" Nigel asked.

"Go home to England, I suppose," Elizabeth answered, rather flatly.

"You want to do?"

"There's nothing else I can do but go."

"Which means," he said shrewdly, "that you don't really want to go?"

"Well"—Elizabeth's hands were clasped again, and the fingers were interlaced nervously—"whether or not I want to go hasn't much to do with it, but my home is in England, and now that my father is dead I've no real excuse for staying in Africa. Besides—"

"Yes?"

"When I came out here I not unnaturally imagined that I would stay and keep house for my father – for at that time"—hastily—"I knew nothing at all of his financial concerns, or really anything at all about him"—rather bitterly—"and I don't think it really crossed my mind that I would go back to England. I have the money for my return fare, of course, but I didn't even take a return ticket." She bit her lip as the sudden realisation of how very much her plans had gone awry swept over her, and how all her dreams and schemes had been doomed from the outset, never to be anything other than dreams and schemes.

But that, perhaps, was the way of life. One nursed a hope for years, and then when it seemed likely to become a reality it crumbled into nothing but dust, and there was only a kind of dull disappointment left behind, and a sensation of bewilderment.

"That is perhaps just as well," Nigel Van Kane observed.

Elizabeth looked at him in faint astonishment.

"You're not really pining to get back to your old life, are you?" he asked. "Your mother and your sisters – well, I should imagine they might manage to survive if you decide to stay out here in Africa!"

Elizabeth felt the colour rush up over her face and neck as she felt his eyes studying her with the old faint look of cynicism back in them, and something else that she did not quite understand.

"But there isn't any question of my staying out here in Africa!"

"Isn't there?" He lightly touched one of her hands where it rested in her lap, turning it over to examine the delicate, flesh-tinted nails. "You don't have to pretend with me, you know," he said, smiling at her in a strange way. "A couple of years ago your father started talking to me about you, but he never mentioned either of your sisters, or your mother. It was Elizabeth he counted upon seeing again one day, and in his eyes, at least, Elizabeth had never done anything to fail him. In fact, he was always conscience-stricken because he felt he had failed you."

Elizabeth felt a mist rise up before her eyes, and she swallowed something in her throat.

"He never failed me," she said, "but we, as a family, failed him!"

"I've told you he completely exonerated you."

"But in your heart you don't exonerate me, any more than you exonerate my mother or my sisters, do you?" she enquired, turning those misty eyes towards him. "Remember that when I first arrived you were prepared to loathe the very sight of me *because* you despised me so much!"

"So you haven't forgotten that," he replied dryly, and stood up suddenly and started to pace up and down in front of her. "Well, if I apologise to you here and now for my mistaken first impression, will you accept the apology? I was probably a bit worked up at that time because I knew how ill your father really was, and it seemed to me that your light-hearted approach to the visit you were paying him was scarcely decent. I didn't, of course, know at that time how much in ignorance you had been kept of the true state of affairs, and it was not until you partly enlightened me when we had that first lunch together in Cape Town that I began to wonder. And after that I wondered still more, for you didn't look the type who would callously neglect a sick father, even if your mother had separated from him years ago. And your father's delight in having you with him – well, that seemed to me to indicate that he had no slightest doubt about you."

She looked down at her hands, where they were clasped in her lap, and she smiled rather tremulously.

"I'm glad, at least, that I was with him on that last night." And then she looked up at him again. "Mr. Van Kane, I've never really thanked you for all that you did for my father – all that you did, apart from maintaining him in comfort in your own home, to make those last years of his life happy and free from care. I know that he was grateful, and that he thought you rather a wonderful person, and I—I …"

"Don't tell me you think me rather a wonderful person, too?"— with a dry note of amusement in his voice.

Elizabeth coloured almost painfully, but she looked at him bravely.

"I think that you behaved in a wonderful fashion to my father, and I would like you to know that I shall never forget your goodness to him – never!"

"Well, at least we seem to have gone a long way towards blotting out altogether our early impressions of one another, don't we?" He came and sat beside her again, and when she refused another cigarette he lighted one himself. He surveyed her through a faint haze of tobacco smoke. "Would you like me to tell you what it was that your father hoped would happen one day? Shall I let you in on one of his secret wishes?"

"You can if you like." But Elizabeth gazed at him suspiciously. "Does it really concern me?"

"It does – and it also concerns me! You see, your father always wanted me to marry one day, because in spite of his own disastrous marriage he was a great believer in it as an institution, and he hoped particularly that you, his youngest and dearest daughter, would contract a happy marriage one of these fine days, too! Oh, I knew perfectly well what the dear old villain had in mind when he pressed for you being allowed to come out and visit him. He showed me your most recent photograph so often, and because I admired it an idea took root in his mind and refused to be dug up."

"You—admired my photograph?" Elizabeth sounded faintly amazed, and she also looked suddenly acutely embarrassed.

"Yes; why not? It was the photograph of a very attractive girl, wasn't it?"

There was a bright sparkle of humour in his eyes, and it confounded her somewhat. But she could see quite clearly what he meant. Any man would admire the photograph of an attractive girl—*any* attractive girl!—and when that girl's father happened to be a very close and rather dear friend he naturally gave voice to his admiration. And her father had misconstrued that admiration and been foolish enough to imagine …!

Oh, but how could he imagine anything of the kind?

She felt herself go hot all over, and under the undisguised amusement in his eyes her cheeks developed painful blushes, and her eyes looked wildly away from him, seeking to fix themselves on anything that was not subjecting her to a faintly derisive scrutiny, and making her feel more appallingly embarrassed than she had ever felt before in her life. If her father had been so simple and naive, at least, she was not! She had to convince him somehow!

"Mr. Van Kane," she began, "I'm quite sure my father was misleading you – he would *never* have been so presumptuous …"

"Wait a minute, wait a minute!" he interrupted her. "Your father was a wise man, and I valued his advice on most things, and I don't see why he should err over matrimony. Besides, he understood me pretty well." He flicked ash from his cigarette into the bed of cannas. "And there comes a time in the lives of most men when they feel that it would be quite a good thing to have a woman in their house running things for them."

"But you have a woman in your house! You have Mrs. McClegg, and she's excellent."

"Quite. But I can't see myself marrying Mrs. McClegg!"

"Are you really seriously thinking about marrying?"

"At the moment I am considering it," he admitted.

Elizabeth still could not bring herself to meet his eyes, for she felt that they were now definitely laughing at her. But what was all this leading up to, and why was he discussing matrimony with her? With her – when there were lovely women in the world, without any ties, like Carol Wainwright, who had known him for quite a long time, and was secretly, Elizabeth was sure, very much interested in him, in spite of the fact that she encouraged the attentions of Mark Temple.

And Elizabeth knew she could never hold a candle to Carol Wainwright.

"Please," she began, "don't you think we ought to go back and join the others?"—partly rising from her chair.

"No." He put his hand on her shoulder and pushed her gently back on to it again. "I want to talk to you, Elizabeth, about your own future, and I want to get something settled. And, to stop beating about the bush, what do you say to my suggestion that you and I do marry one another? And then I can take you back to Groote Kloof as its mistress, and you won't have to worry your head about return passages to England, and beginning life again in the bosom of your family!"

For a moment Elizabeth was so utterly astounded that she could say nothing, and he smiled at her rallyingly.

"Well?"

"But why—why should you want to marry me?" she got out at last. "And why—?"

"Why should I assume that you would find the idea of marriage to me attractive? Well, I don't – quite honestly, I'm merely being extremely practical and putting to you all the practical advantages of such a union, as the Victorians would phrase it." And before she could even open her lips again he went on: "Naturally I don't expect you to pretend to me that you're in love with me, for you've seen so little of me that that could hardly be the case, but your father was quite sure you are entirely heartwhole, so you're not yearning to marry someone else." Elizabeth gazed at him with wide, fascinated eyes, and he smiled into them rather whimsically. "I have a particular reason for wanting to do what your father wished, and I'd like to see you settled and happy, Elizabeth. So what do you say?"

"What can I say?" She moistened her lips slightly. "It sounds completely fantastic to me."

"But I don't think it's at all fantastic. And one of these days we might develop quite a liking for one another!"

One of these days …! Something inside Elizabeth started to tremble suddenly, and a feeling of breathlessness rushed up into her throat as his dark eyes continued to gaze at her, and they were only a bare few inches from her own. She remembered the night when she had stepped on what she had imagined was a snake in the garden of Groote Kloof, and how his arms had held her close to him, and how thankful she had been for the support of those arms. Some magnetism had flowed from him to her in those moments, even in the midst of her unreasoning panic, that had astonished her when she thought about it afterwards, and when she thought about it now that strange sensation of breathlessness increased.

"Out of bad beginnings it is possible for good endings to be arrived at," he told her, still smiling. "And somehow I believe you liked Groote Kloof. You didn't really want to leave it when you came here, did you?"

"No," she admitted, because that was no more than the truth. "I don't think I did."

"Can't you be quite sure about it?"

She nodded her head suddenly, looking at him gravely.

"Yes; I can be quite sure. But perhaps that was because my father—" She broke off, biting her lip.

"Perhaps it was," he agreed, more dryly. "For you Groote Kloof will always have associations with your father, won't it? But tell me – do you want to go home to England?"

Elizabeth mentally reviewed her life in England – her job in an antique shop where she had been quite happy, but never anything more positive. Her home in the outer suburbs, and the day-to-day routine there. Her mother's interests, and her friends, had been more or less forced upon her as her interests and her friends, also. She had never been permitted any individuality, and perhaps that was why she had always secretly yearned to break away. And having broken away, having cut herself off in spirit as well as everything else from the life she had once led, could she go back to it and pick up the threads and be merely complacently happy again?

She took one quick look at the man beside her, with his keen, somewhat arrogant face, and despite the fact that the chin was ruthless, and the mouth hard—or she had seen it looking very hard indeed on one or two occasions!—she knew that she could not bear to go back to England and know that she would never see him again.

And then, as she suddenly realised what she was thinking, her face again grew hot, and she looked away from him quickly in case, with his extraordinary shrewdness, he should be able to read her thoughts. And if he read them he would learn, probably to his astonishment, that it was not only because it had associations with her father that Groote Kloof had become desirable to her. There was another reason …

"Do you?" he repeated, suddenly sounding impatient.

Elizabeth tore her glance from the bed of cannas and looked back at him again, and then away.

"No," she said truthfully, her fingers clutching at her belt.

"Do you want to stay in Africa?"

"I would like to see—more of Africa!"

His lips curved strangely.

"Could you bear to become my wife? Or does the idea revolt you?"

Oh, thought Elizabeth, if only that discomposing feeling of excitement would stop pervading her whole body at the very thought of becoming his wife! If only she could believe that his suggestion had not some ulterior motive behind it – it was such an amazing suggestion!

"I can't imagine why you should pick on me for a wife," she said suddenly, slowly, still not looking at him. "You know practically nothing about me."

"That's probably a good thing," he replied, rather lazily. "It will give me something to do, to learn what I do not know about you!"

She stole a glance at his features, and their expression baffled her. Suddenly he smiled at her more softly.

"Are you waiting to hear me say that I love you – and that *that* is the reason why I want to marry you? Because I'm not going to say anything of the kind! I've already told you that one day – one day, perhaps, we may grow to like one another very much, but in the meantime all you have to do is to weigh up all the advantages to yourself, set them against the disadvantages, and decide what the outcome of that must be. If you *don't* consider the advantages outweigh the disadvantages, then we'll say no more about it!"

It was the strangest proposal, and under ordinary circumstances Elizabeth would have been tempted to ignore it altogether. But these were not ordinary circumstances. If she refused him she had to go away from him—right away out of his life!—and if she accepted him – what sort of life could she expect ?

She stood up suddenly, looking very slender and young and grave, as she faced him. There was also a new sort of rather touching dignity about her.

"Since you must realise that the advantages all lie with me," she said, "there is one thing I would like to ask you." She paused. "Are you doing this—have you asked me to marry you to—spite someone else?"

He looked amused, and then he shook his head.

"You're older than I thought you were, Elizabeth. But no, I shall not be doing anything to 'spite' anyone else. You can be quite easy in your mind about that."

"Then why?"

He continued to smile, rather in the old mocking fashion.

"Let's say that I like the idea of marrying you!"

Elizabeth declined to allow her gravity to slip from her. He stood up suddenly and spoke more curtly, turning away from her in the path.

"Oh, forget all about it for the time being," he advised. "There's no hurry, and important decisions can't be rushed. Come on, let's get back to the house!"

But, all at once, Elizabeth knew that she had to make the decision there and then, and she made it. She put out a hand and touched his sleeve, and he turned at once. He looked at her with one eyebrow raised.

"I—" Elizabeth found that her voice was not very strong. "If you really meant it, I—I think I—"

"Yes?"—watching her coolly.

She struggled on: "If you really meant what you said, and you weren't just joking – then—then I have already decided—"

"To marry me?" He helped her out, but there was no change in his tone. "Good!" he exclaimed, as if she had just agreed to go out to dinner with him, or to go for a drive. "I was certainly not joking, because I'm not accustomed to joke about things of that nature. And now we'll go and break the news to the others, and witness their reactions – which I'm quite sure will be many and varied!"

## Chapter Ten

There was no doubt about the reactions of the others, but they were not particularly varied. Only Mark Temple betrayed no surprise, and he looked at Elizabeth with a rather quizzical expression on his face. Her hostess's face went suddenly almost completely blank, and then she turned to Elizabeth and wound her arms about her and kissed her effusively.

"My dear," she said softly, "you *are* a deep one! I'd no idea there was anything at all between you, and now you spring this on us! But how romantic! A shipboard love-affair culminates in marriage! Delightful!"

But there was no delight in her eyes as she studied the tall, assured figure of Nigel Van Kane, lounging negligently in the opening of the long windows, with the sunlight behind him. His eyes, as they met her own, were inscrutable, and hers were mysterious, hard blue pools. She smiled with her over-reddened lips.

"Darling," she said to him, very gently, "Groote Kloof will have a mistress now whom Mrs. McClegg can train for you. She'll love doing that, I'm sure – and Elizabeth is so young that she won't mind being instructed!"

After that there was no other conversation but that which definitely bore on the wedding, and everyone was anxious to know how soon it would be. Elizabeth felt as if she was moving and living in a dream as she listened to the quips and the chatter on all sides of her and when she heard Van Kane offer the piece of information that it would probably be very soon she wondered how soon she would wake up and discover that it was all a most unlikely dream.

He stayed to dinner that night, but his manner to her was exactly the same as it had always been, save in those first few days of their acquaintance when it had been hostile. Before he left, he took her out into the veranda and told her that he proposed collecting her the following day, Christmas Day, and driving her in his car out to Groote Kloof, where they could receive the felicitations of Mrs. McClegg and sample her Christmas dinner, which would be provided in the middle of the day.

"And as you've never had an opportunity to look over the farm I'll show it to you. Remember you're going to become the wife of a wine grower, and the wife of a wine grower must know something about the way her husband amasses his income!"

He looked down at her as she stood before him in the wide, moonlit veranda, hearing the word "husband" fall on her ears and finding it quite impossible to believe that as the result of their afternoon's conversation that was what he was shortly to become – her husband!

There was a bemused look on her face, with its wide, dove-like grey eyes, and he knew she was trying to take a firm grasp of reality as she gazed up at him and recollected how astonished all those friends of his had been—including her hostess, when she first heard the news!—because he had decided to marry a twenty-two-year-old English girl with nothing very striking about her in the way of looks, although she was pleasing enough if one avoided comparison with anyone like Carol Wainwright; a girl whose father had been his protégé.

Carol was probably right, they thought, when she talked about a shipboard love-affair, because otherwise the two knew little or nothing about one another, and had had no opportunity to get to know one another. But they knew one another well enough to marry!

The whole affair was extraordinary, unless it was the attraction of opposites. The girl was unsure of herself, shy, but attractive in a way that would make some men feel they wanted to protect her. The man in the case was dark and strong and arrogant, and he could do all the protecting that was necessary if he felt like it.

"Don't look as if you're not quite sure whether you're awake or dreaming," Nigel murmured, before he said good night. "You are awake, you know!" He put out a finger and lifted her chin and smiled at her. "Be ready when I call for you tomorrow, and I promise you a pleasant day."

And it was a pleasant day, from the moment that he and his big car arrived at the foot of the veranda steps, and Carol and the remains of her house-party waved them goodbye while they lay in long chairs on the veranda. Elizabeth was glad when they slipped between the gates, and the road to Groote Kloof lay ahead of them. She knew excitement at the thought of returning to Groote Kloof, and she was looking forward to meeting Mrs. McClegg once more. But when they were midway between Elandfontein and Groote Kloof, Nigel stopped the car and presented her with a small parcel, which she opened with some astonishment.

"Christmas comes but once a year," he observed, in his dry voice, "and I thought it mustn't be allowed to pass without providing you with some small memento of today. And, incidentally, it will serve another purpose as well."

Elizabeth looked at him rather doubtfully, and then removed the paper wrappings from the square ring-case. Inside, when she lifted the lid, was an unusually cut sapphire of great beauty and depth of colour, mounted in platinum, nestling on a bed of velvet. She uttered a little gasp of pleasure when she first gazed at the stone, but when the man she was to marry said curtly: "Put it on," she hesitated for a moment.

"Put it on," Van Kane repeated, and as she made no move to do so, but seemed mesmerised by the beauty of the stone, he removed the ring from its case and slid it on the slender third finger of her left hand. The size was perfect, and it surprised her so much that she exclaimed aloud in astonishment: "Why, it fits perfectly! Absolutely perfectly!"

"Of course it does," he agreed quietly. "But as you left one of your gloves behind in the room you occupied at Groote Kloof that is not really surprising."

But what was surprising was that he had purchased the ring before he had asked her to marry him, and that surely indicated that he had been very sure of her answer when he did make his proposal. She glanced sideways at the impassive face behind the wheel, with eyes fixed steadily on the road ahead, and she wondered … why had he been so sure of her answer!

Mrs. McClegg came out on to the front stoep to welcome them when they arrived at Groote Kloof, and from the beaming quality of her smile Elizabeth gathered that the news had already been imparted to her that the house was to receive a mistress, and that far from feeling any resentment she was inclined to welcome the idea. When she got Elizabeth alone for a few minutes upstairs in the room where the girl had once slept, and where she went to tidy herself before lunch, she confessed to her that although somewhat astonished she was more pleased than she could say that it was Elizabeth who was to become Mrs. Van Kane.

"I don't mind telling you now, Miss Elizabeth," she said, with her distinct Scottish burr, "but there have been moments when I could have sworn that it was going to be that other one, and she and I would never see eye to eye."

"That other one?" Elizabeth inquired, looking at her in faint bewilderment. "Do you mean—?"

"Mrs. Wainwright." Mrs. McClegg uttered the name, and then tightened her lips. "I know you're staying with her, and perhaps I oughtn't to say these things, but if ever anyone ran after Master Nigel she did. Even before that husband of hers got himself killed—"

"Oh!" Elizabeth exclaimed, and went to the dressing-table and patted her hair into place in the hopes that she could put a stop to this sort of conversation. She opened her powder compact and hastily powdered her face, but Mrs. McClegg was not to be entirely silenced.

"And that's another mystery we shall never really know the rights of. Mr. Wainwright and Mr. Temple had gone after game together, and they were alone except for their porters. And Mr. Wainwright – Bryn, as Mrs. Wainwright always called him – was the last man you'd ever imagine would allow himself to be mauled and killed by a lion, but that's what happened to him. One of the best shots that ever crossed Africa from north to south – that's what his reputation was before ever he met and married his wife – and he and Mr. Temple were always going off somewhere together. And what we would all like to know is *what was Mr. Temple doing at the time of the accident?"*

Mrs. McClegg paused significantly, and Elizabeth felt suddenly disturbed. Surely it was not true that people wondered about anything of the kind, and if they did it must be very unpleasant for Mark Temple. Certainly there was nothing in his demeanour that suggested his conscience was not absolutely clear – in fact, he was one of the most careless and carefree of men, or so he seemed. And Carol Wainwright extended to him a considerable amount of friendship, which meant that she, for once, had every confidence in him. In fact, she must have a great deal of confidence, since she allowed him to make use of her house as a kind of unofficial and free hotel whenever he happened to be in her neighbourhood.

"I'd better go downstairs and not keep Mr. Van Kane waiting for lunch," the visitor said, backing hastily in the direction of the door. And then, in order to soften her obvious method of cutting short the housekeeper's local reminiscences, she added, smiling: "As it's Christmas, I expect it's rather a special lunch, and you won't want it spoiled."

Mrs. McClegg beamed back at her, not objecting in the least to having her flow of suspicions stemmed.

"Oh, as to that, I have gone to rather a lot of trouble to make sure you'll like it," she admitted. "When the master told me last night that he was bringing you out here today I thought, seeing you're so newly out from England, and likely to be feeling a bit homesick— with the poor doctor so recently passed on, and all!—that I'd have everything as English as possible, so that you wouldn't feel quite so strange."

"That's very nice of you, Mrs McClegg," Elizabeth replied gratefully. And when she descended to the dining room and found that the dining table, apart from the vase of exotic blooms which formed its centrepiece, was decorated in much the same manner as she was accustomed to see Christmas dinner tables at home decorated, she was touched by the evidence of Mrs. McClegg's desire to please. And the dinner itself was just such a dinner as she was accustomed to eating at home at this season, with turkey, plum pudding, mince pies and all the usual trimmings. But for the absence of scarlet berries and glossy festoons of laurel and mistletoe, and the fact that the sunlight outside the windows was fierce and warm, she might easily have imagined that she was at home in England, with the pattern of her life not greatly altered from the lines it had presented a year before.

But she had only to lift her eyes to the man seated opposite her to realise, with a little shock, that everything was indeed altered. Obeying some impulse she could not in the least understand now that it was past, she had agreed to marry him only the day before, and the full significance of what she had agreed to do had not yet been borne in on her. She was not even certain that she *had* agreed to marry him – or, if she had, whether he had taken her seriously – but there was no doubt about the reality of his ring on her finger.

But even that did not bind her to him. It was merely a ring, and he had described it as a Christmas present when he gave it to her. But every time her eyes dropped to it she felt his eyes following her own, and when she looked up at him again he seemed to be smiling slightly.

She was not quite sure what sort of a smile it was.

During the meal he behaved as a very attentive host, and if she had felt a little less vague in her mind as to what was happening to her just then she might have found him an entertaining one. He certainly put himself out to be, keeping the ball of conversation rolling between them. And perhaps because he had the feeling that while they sat there at the table in the cream-walled dining room she was recalling that last night of her father's life when he had sat there with them, he made no attempt to spin out the meal, and suggested that they removed to the front stoep for their coffee.

And again it seemed odd to her that she should be sitting there close to him on the broad stoep and pouring his coffee when there was no one else with them to take away the strangeness, or make it seem slightly more normal.

Later in the afternoon he drove her in his car over a part of the estate, but as it was a holiday and there was no actual work being done anywhere, the secrets of a wine-growing farm were not opened up to her, and she saw only the well-tended vines and the acres and acres of his land that were devoted to the cultivation of fruit. The varieties of South African fruit were far greater than she had imagined, and it seemed to her extraordinary that in December peaches, apricots pineapples, figs, plums, pears and papaws should be rioting everywhere. Wherever she looked there were trees climbing the slopes, silhouetted against the skyline; and where there were no fruit trees there were the long, neat vineyards lying open to the sun, with magnificent purple grapes swelling and sweetening in the hot, still air.

In the blaze of the afternoon sun they travelled through this fruitful valley, and sometimes when Elizabeth looked backwards she caught a glimpse of white, gracious Groote Kloof standing protected by its tall trees, and looking out to the blue line of mountains.

Quite late in the afternoon they returned to the house for tea, and then Elizabeth went upstairs to her old room to wash and tidy herself. When she went down to the stoep again she was looking cool and refreshed, with a warm glow in her cheeks like the glow on the sides of a peach, her fair hair curling softly about her face, and her white linen dress still immaculate.

Nigel was standing beside a table that supported a tray of drinks, and he looked up at her and asked her what she would like to have. Somewhat nervously she seated herself near the edge of a chair and said that she would like a long glass of iced lime juice. She was aware that Mrs. McClegg was no longer on duty, and that she had gone off to visit friends who lived not so very far away, and Muemba seemed to be nowhere in evidence. The house behind them lay quiet and still, while in front of them the green lawns turned to emerald in the last vivid light of the day, and the only sound was the chanting of the cicadas.

A tiny, thoughtful smile curved the man's lips as he studied the girl's bent head, and after a few moments the smile stole up into his eyes. He could tell by her attitude that she was by no means entirely at her ease with him.

"I thought I'd drive you back to Elandfontein in time for dinner," he said, "but in the meantime we'll have a little talk!"

Elizabeth barely raised her eyes to his face, but her pulses leapt suddenly and uneasily. So it was coming, she thought, the moment that she had been vaguely expecting to draw nearer all day! Their lunch together, their tour of the vineyards and a large portion of his estate, had merely kept the moment at bay, but it was refusing to be kept at bay any longer, and she had to deal with that moment calmly. She had to remember that only the day before she had received a proposal of marriage, and she had accepted that proposal.

You couldn't do that sort of thing without facing up to the consequences!

The man she had agreed to marry sat down suddenly in a chair facing her and stretched his long limbs comfortably in a relaxed attitude. The smile remained in his eyes, but behind it something that was cold and a little forbidding started to spread slowly, in a somewhat sinister fashion. The coldness was noticeable in his voice when he spoke rather abruptly: "Regretting your decision already?" he inquired, examining the bright tip of his cigarette. "You'd probably like to tell me that you've changed your mind and you don't think marrying me is such a good idea after all?"

Elizabeth looked up at him, almost startled, for the tone of his voice was equivalent to a whiplash. She felt the hot, faintly indignant colour sting her cheeks.

"Why do you say that?" she asked.

"Because I've been feeling all day that your rash promise yesterday has been hanging over you like a cloud from the moment you woke up this morning. That you'd rather like me to say I didn't mean it yesterday, and let you off lightly. But I did mean it, and I haven't any intention at all of letting you off!"

Elizabeth set down her glass of lime juice very slowly and carefully on the little table near to her. She looked across at him and met his eyes and felt perfectly capable of going on meeting his eyes indefinitely, for what he had just said to her had succeeded in making her angry. For one thing it was not true that she had regretted her decision, and she had no intention of going back on her word. The only thing that had been troubling her all day was the sensation of unreality that had prevented her from understanding clearly whether she was irrevocably committed to marrying Nigel Van Kane, and whether his proposal had indeed been made in earnest. His behaviour all day had done nothing to help her to get a clear grasp of the situation, or a clear picture of their relationship, but his contemptuous tone now put her on her mettle.

"As a matter of fact," she confessed, "I am not at all sure whether you were serious yesterday, or whether perhaps *you* would rather I did not take you seriously! And if that is what you would prefer you have only to say so."

Somewhat to her surprise an instantaneous change came over his face, and in place of the forbidding look, one of the most genuinely amused smiles she had ever seen in his eyes banished the suggestion of cold criticism, and the corners of his mouth twitched upwards with amusement.

"In that case," he said, "we're back where we were when we started off this morning, and I give you my solemn word that it has never been my practice to propose marriage to a young woman of your age *without* meaning precisely what I said at the time! As a point of interest it might also give you reassurance to hear that I have never offered marriage to any young woman until I offered it to you yesterday, and from that confession alone you might gather that I am remarkably cautious! And being cautious I always put my foot down very warily, and *never* where I might regret having placed it!"

Elizabeth could not prevent a most attractive but rather wild blush from spreading all over her face and brow as his amused eyes studied her, but inside herself she was considerably amazed by the confession he had just made. For a man of his age, even if he had never actually proposed marriage to another woman, must at least have felt some interest at some time or another – or some woman *must* have felt interest in him!

"Then you really do want me to—to marry you?" she stammered awkwardly, no longer able to meet his eyes.

"Of course! And I shall take it as a personal affront if you go back on your word!"

"I have no intention of going back on it," she answered, asking herself at the same time why – *why* did he want to marry her? And why had he picked on her in any case? It couldn't be solely because of his affection for her father, and because he had been able to interpret aright her father's wishes! A man who was wary about taking unwise steps didn't contract marriage just because of a whim!

She wished, as the night began to come down with a rush, and she began for the first time to feel vaguely uncertain in her own mind, knowing at last that she really was committed to a highly problematical future, and that she might be taking a very, very unwise step, that she could learn something of what was passing in his mind, and that the real Nigel Van Kane and all his secret thoughts were not as completely hidden from her as the garden, with all its profusion of growth and its daytime brilliance, would soon be hidden from her eyes.

He must have sensed that, although she was not in any way weakening concerning the decision she had made, a sudden ingredient of timorousness – of a yearning for reassurance, any kind of reassurance – had entered her mind and her heart (just as completely unknown to him as his was to her!) for he stood up suddenly and went across to her and poured her out a glass of sherry and put it into her hand instead of the lime juice which she had barely tasted.

"Drink this," he said, with a new note of gentleness in his voice, "and don't bother yourself any more about whether you are doing the right thing or not. Just take it that you are."

When she obediently sipped the sherry he took the glass from her and set it down on the table. Then he said quietly: "We'll get married very soon, as there seems to be nothing to wait for. And you can come over here and go through the place with Mrs. McClegg and decide upon any alterations you would like to have made. At present the place has the atmosphere of a purely bachelor establishment, but if you are to live here we must remedy that."

"I think everything is very nice as it is," she said, somewhat unsteadily.

"Do you?" He seemed to be peering at her through the gloom. "Well, it might suit some women, but you're the ultra-feminine type, so I'm not sure. But we can go into all that in the course of the coming week. Do you want me to write home to your mother and announce myself as her future son-in-law?"

The idea struck Elizabeth as so completely unnecessary that she stared at him in surprise. And yet, once she began to think of it, she supposed that her mother had a right to be informed of her plans, and Kay and Christine would probably think it amazing that she was getting married to soon. They might even think they ought to be invited to the wedding!

The idea suddenly disturbed her.

"Must you?" she murmured. "Do you have to?"

He smiled rather grimly.

"I certainly don't have to, and as you're of age you don't have to, either. But I think your father would have wished it, somehow. And I think we'd both like to do what he would have wished."

"Yes." Elizabeth felt a sudden little glow of warmth. At least that was one thing that would always provide a tie between them – their mutual affection for her father, and her father, she knew, would never have erred when it came to doing the right thing. "But it won't give you any pleasure to write to my mother, will it?" she asked suddenly, shrewdly. "You really haven't much time for her, have you?"

"Much less than I once thought I had for you," he told her, smiling rather whimsically as they went down the steps to his car.

The night was wrapping them sensuously about as they climbed into the car, and the stars were like brilliant eyes overhead. Elizabeth lay back against the well-sprung seat and felt all at once almost completely relaxed. He was thoughtful, she knew now, this man she was to marry, and he did not shirk an unpleasant task merely because it was unpleasant. The letter to her mother, for instance – he would probably hate writing it, despising her as he did, but he would write it.

She looked back upon the day just ended, and she knew that it had been an extraordinarily peaceful day, and but for her feeling of vagueness she might have enjoyed it. In a way she *had* enjoyed it.

Suddenly she said shyly: "It's been a very nice day – thank you!"

He was just starting up the engine, and he smiled down at her.

"I promise you it won't be the only nice day we'll spend together!"

# Chapter Eleven

They were married in Cape Town three weeks after Christmas had come and gone.

The three weeks devoted to preparation were never afterwards clearly recollected by Elizabeth, but she knew that they flew by in a rush and whirl of shopping and collecting all the items for a trousseau under the supervision of Carol Wainwright, who displayed a surprising amount of enthusiasm for her task.

It was surprising to Elizabeth because, from the very beginning of their acquaintance, she had suspected that Carol had never really approved of her being invited as a guest to Groote Kloof, and that although she had thought well of Dr. Ransome, his daughter, with her youth and inexperience, was another matter altogether. Carol did not really enjoy the society of young and inexperienced members of her own sex, and when one of her old and particular friends took to paying noticeable attentions to that youth and inexperience, Elizabeth had been certain that she would not approve. She had hidden her disapproval under a screen of professed concern for the girl herself, and the menace of her good name if she went on accepting hospitality in a bachelor establishment. But Elizabeth had been shrewd enough to recognise that that was not really what worried her.

Now Carol, having overcome the shock of the announcement of an engagement between Nigel and his late protégé's daughter, declared that she thought it an excellent thing for Elizabeth, and added that she thought it was high time Nigel, too, settled down, and provided his home with a mistress.

"We had all made up our minds that Nigel was one of those people who would never get married," she told Elizabeth, the first time the two of them were alone after the Christmas holidays, "but it would seem that we were all wrong." She smiled rather oddly at Elizabeth, studying the outline of the delicate face, lighted by the uncomplicated grey eyes. "I wonder what it is about you, my dear, that has brought about such a ready capitulation? Do you generally have this effect on the men of your acquaintance?"

Elizabeth denied hastily that she did anything of the kind, and Carol, lying back and smoking one of her specially blended cigarettes – she favoured a mixture of Turkish and Virginian tobaccos – allowed her smile to become a little more openly speculative.

"It could be your youth," she said. "Some men, especially when they happen to be a good deal older, do fall for an absence of sophistication and an almost complete lack of poise. But remember, my dear, such things have been known to pall before now—at any rate, after a time!—and if you want to keep a man on his toes you'll have to begin to grow up and keep pace with him and his interests just as soon as you discover that the first fine careless rapture is showing signs of wear and tear!"

She smiled in the way she could do when she was conscious that her words might have a rather sharp edge, and lent forward and ran a finger lightly down Elizabeth's smooth cheek.

But Elizabeth wondered, as she had wondered more than once before when her hostess expressed herself in a similar manner. And she knew she would be glad when the moment arrived for her to leave Elandfontein. There was something about the place that brooded, and was not really at all pleased because she was a guest beneath its roof.

But she could not deny appreciation when Mrs. Wainwright introduced her to her own dressmaker and hairdresser, and took such an active interest in her purchases for her wedding that everything she acquired was exactly right for her. Mrs. Wainwright, who had a natural flair for dress, knew what suited Elizabeth, and saw to it that nothing that did not suit Elizabeth was made part of her new outfit. The one thing which seriously worried Elizabeth was that Carol, with her own comfortable income, had no idea of the necessity for sometimes practising economy, and she was a little horrified when she was persuaded into extravagances as a result of the sheer determined enthusiasm of her hostess.

When she protested that she could not really afford these things Carol at first looked amazed, and then laughed at her in amusement.

"My dear," she reminded her, "aren't you marrying a man with enough money to burn if he felt like it? And if you're short of cash, you have but to ask him for some and he'll advance it."

Elizabeth felt a flame of indignation sweep over her. She could not be sure that Mrs. Wainwright was speaking seriously, but she strongly suspected that she was not merely indulging in sarcasm. There was a bright sparkle of humour in the lovely blue eyes as they surveyed Elizabeth, and there was a look which also suggested that Elizabeth was quite extraordinarily young for her years.

"But you don't really imagine I would borrow money from— from anyone!" the latter got out at last, with the indignant colour flaming high in her cheeks. "Least of all from a man I—"

"From a man you hardly know, darling?" The words were soft and drawling.

"I was going to say, from a man I'm expecting to marry," Elizabeth concluded more quietly, and with a suddenly acquired touch of noticeable dignity. "After I've married him no doubt he'll provide me with funds when I need them, but I don't expect him to do so *before* I marry him!"

Carol laughed softly.

"How quaint!" she exclaimed. "How deliciously quaint!" And then, with a cold steely brightness replacing the humour in her eyes: "You have been brought up correctly, haven't you, my dear? Never a foot wrong! But sometimes it's possible to miscalculate – sometimes the cleverest amongst us makes a mistake?"

There it was again! That sudden, almost vicious little flame of dislike, rising up this time in a more open manner than ever before. Elizabeth was all at once appalled by the nakedness of the enmity which looked at her out of the violet-blue eyes under the extraordinary fringe of thick black eyelashes. She felt herself go cold inside, and for a moment she waited, expecting something more – some further revelation that would disturb her still more. Some accusation that she was the sort of girl who made use of her youth and her apparent inexperience—her gently-brought-up façade!—to entrap a man who had a great deal to offer.

But after that moment of somewhat breathless waiting Mrs. Wainwright recovered all her usual complete good humour, and she actually laughed again, lightly.

"Poor Elizabeth!" she exclaimed. "What were you expecting me to accuse you of? You looked quite frightened!"

And then she suggested that they went and had tea and called it a day so far as shopping was concerned. And all the way home in the car she chatted quite lightly and blithely to Elizabeth, being her most charming self, and obviously doing her best to erase from Elizabeth's mind that doubt which had entered it.

But Elizabeth did not recover quite so quickly. She was quiet for the remainder of that day, and she made up her mind that there was to be no more heedless expenditure in connection with her wedding outfit, and that what she could not afford she would do without. Whatever her hostess might have to say on the subject, and however persuasive she might be, she would be firm and refuse to be tempted.

That night Nigel came to dinner with them, and he looked at Elizabeth rather keenly, as if something unusually subdued and repressed in her manner did not escape him.

Since Christmas Day, when they had lunched together, and had spent the whole day together at Groote Kloof, Elizabeth had stopped wilfully deceiving herself, and she knew that his comings and goings were amongst the most important things that could happen to her in life. Before long they would be so important that if they ever ceased – and the very thought of anything of that kind ever happening made her feel as if her supply of breath had come to an end, and she had been brought up sharply by some kind of rude jolt – then she could not imagine how she would feel, or how she would react. She supposed she would go on as she had gone on before he ever came into her life, but there would be no savour in her existence, and it would be rather like a dreary waste stretching in front of her.

She knew now why she had agreed to marry him – because she had *had* to agree! To have let him go, to have refused him, which would certainly have been more dignified when he had never once professed any sort of attachment for her, was something she could see clearly now she could not have done, and the constant wonder to her was that she had ever had the opportunity to accept him for a husband.

Since that day at Groote Kloof he had never once reverted to his old arrogant attitude towards her. Sometimes he was surprisingly gentle, and she always found him considerate. He had written to her mother in England and told her about their approaching marriage, and when he received a gushing and fulsome reply he did not disclose the fact that it slightly revolted him, but showed it to Elizabeth with a faint smile on his lips.

Elizabeth, reading between the lines, understood plainly her mother's reactions, and what she expected from the future and a married daughter. If she could not be at the latter's wedding, at least she expected to be invited to stay with her and her new son-in-law at no very distant date after their marriage had taken place, and Kay and Christine, in letters which were almost as fulsome, hinted plainly at their own very natural desire to see their sister's new home, when she was installed in it, and make the acquaintance of her husband, just as soon as it was absolutely convenient.

Kay and Christine could well afford to pay their own fares out to South Africa, and it was obvious that the thought that had taken possession of both girls' minds was that if a girl like Elizabeth, young, inexperienced and only moderately attractive compared with themselves, could acquire a husband of satisfying means and reputation so soon after her arrival in Africa, surely they could!

Elizabeth felt inclined to blush for the obvious angling for invitations to stay with her once she was married which showed through all three letters, and it was only when she realised that Nigel was amused rather than anything else that the blushes began to subside.

"Don't worry," he said. "One of these days I might find it interesting to meet the other members of your family."

The plans for their wedding went ahead without any sort of hitch because for one thing they were severely simple. Following the civil ceremony there was to be lunch at a hotel in Cape Town, and then the couple were to leave by air for the northern part of the country where Van Kane had another small mixed farm which he occasionally visited, and where he decided they would spend what was officially to be described as a honeymoon.

Apparently the farm was rather remote; it had few of the amenities of Groote Kloof, but it stood in high, healthy country, and to visit it would provide Elizabeth with an opportunity to see something more of Africa. Once she reached there Elizabeth discovered that it had another advantage which had not been mentioned to her beforehand, and that was that the place was staffed entirely by local labour, and there was no one like Mrs. McClegg, with her native Scottish shrewdness and her keen powers of observation, to be there when the honeymooners arrived.

But before they arrived there was all the curious, repressed excitement of the last day at Elandfontein to be lived through, and Elizabeth felt that it was a day that would never draw to its end.

Mark Temple, who had deserted them for a few days, was there to lunch, and it seemed to Elizabeth that his eyes watched her with a mixture of speculation and amusement during the meal. No doubt, she thought, he was wondering how this marriage was going to turn out, and being of a somewhat cynical turn of mind he had probably decided that it would be no better and no worse than most of them.

Carol had alternate moods of excessive sweetness and sudden little bursts of irritability, which she vented for the most part on Mark – who accepted most of her moods with equanimity, and was apparently never upset by any of them.

Nigel arrived for dinner, and afterwards Elizabeth went out on to the veranda with him while the other two played a card game in the room behind them.

The night was hot and breathless, and over their heads an orange moon sailed serenely into the star-studded sky – that brilliant African moon against whom Elizabeth had once been half-mockingly warned! But tonight she was too nervous to be affected by moonlight or anything else. The following day she would exchange her status as an unmarried young woman for the status of a wife, and whether or not she was doing a wise thing only the future would be able to tell her.

Beside her the man she was to marry seemed all at once to have become a quiet and thoughtful stranger. He was leaning against the veranda rail and staring out across the garden as it became dimly visible to their eyes. Elizabeth, who stood beside him, could feel his shoulder lightly brushing hers, but in spite of this contact she felt they might be miles away. She longed, in a suddenly panic-stricken way, for some sort of actual contact. She longed to bolster up her dwindling supply of confidence, but the man did not seem to be aware that she had any urgent need of this kind.

All at once his voice spoke to her, and it was measured and cool, and a little dry.

"It's not too late," he said, "if you want to change your mind! Remember that by this time tomorrow night it will be too late!"

Elizabeth drew a long, faintly shuddering breath. Her fingers gripped the veranda rail.

"And if I said that I didn't want to go through with it at this late stage, what would you say?"

"I would neither say nor do anything to prevent you from backing out!" His voice, now, was almost painfully quiet. "So just go ahead and give the matter a good think, and try and forget about me while you do so. Try and pretend even that I don't exist."

"In that case, I wouldn't be contemplating marrying you tomorrow, would I?" she murmured, with something like a suddenly shaky smile in the words.

"No." She saw his white teeth for a moment, glimmering through the darkness. "You wouldn't."

There was silence between them for several seconds, and it was a silence that pressed upon Elizabeth like the darkness of the night before the moon rose. It was a waiting silence, full of tension, pregnant with all sorts of possibilities, unendurable if it had gone on for long. And she knew that the man beside her was as conscious of it as she was, and she could sense rather than feel that he was holding himself very stiffly as he leaned there beside her against the rail. His head was almost rigidly upright as he stared at the moon.

"Of course I shall go through with it," Elizabeth got out at last, and Nigel Van Kane relaxed almost with the words, and again she caught the glimmer of his white teeth through the darkness as he smiled.

"Brave Elizabeth!" he exclaimed.

Elizabeth wondered whether he was mocking her, or whether he was serious. And then she turned her head a little and looked up at him, and in the slowly spreading radiance of the moon she could see that his eyes were gazing directly down at her. They were deep and dark like the velvety depth and darkness of the sky above their heads, and those little golden lights that usually swam in them were no longer to be seen.

"And you're quite, quite sure?"

"Yes. I'm quite, quite sure!"

To her surprise he suddenly reached out and took both her hands and drew them up against him, holding them lightly against the lapels of his dinner-jacket. Her fingers felt like imprisoned birds as they rested there against the fine white material of his coat, and the dark fingers that covered them were warm and strong and vital, taking possession of her somehow.

"Brave Elizabeth!" he exclaimed again, and then he smiled at her gently and bent and lightly kissed the top of her head before announcing that he must really take his departure.

# Chapter Twelve

The following day Elizabeth was glad of the support which Carol Wainwright gave her. All the moodiness of the day before was gone, and she was encouraging and soothing and confidence-inspiring all at the same time, and Elizabeth felt that without her she would never have comported herself in the manner that was expected of her.

After the civil ceremony – which was over so soon that Elizabeth thought vaguely that it could not really have done anything very much to change the way of her life – they had lunch at a hotel in Cape Town that looked right out to the blue Atlantic rollers, curling in line after line on the smooth golden sand. The haze of summer lay over the hotel balconies and the gardens gay with bougainvillea and hibiscus, and the neat white villas and clear-cut blocks of flats that also fronted the ocean. Their table was in the window, and Elizabeth could see all this as she gazed out through the sparkling glass, over the massed flowers that formed the table's decoration.

She was glad, when she found out where they were to have lunch, that it was not the hotel where she had had her first lunch in Cape Town with the man who was now her husband. Her memories of that day, and the opinion that had been held of her at that time, were not the kind to recall on a wedding day, and perhaps that was one reason why Van Kane, who thought of most things, had not selected the hotel.

He looked, however, almost exactly as she had seen him on that day; immaculate in a thin suit, his dark face austere and his expression withdrawn as if the thoughts that dwelt behind his remote dark eyes were serious ones. Mark Temple, on the other hand, who had undertaken the role of best man, was full of lively conversation and witty sallies that were directed mostly at the newly-married pair, but sometimes at Carol Wainwright, who seemed perfectly able to bear them with composure, and not infrequently returned them with a brand of humour that was just a little more caustic.

Carol was looking as if she ought to be the bride, Elizabeth thought, in an outfit that had cost far more than anything she herself owned. It was of a misty lavender shade, worn with white accessories, and the flattering hue of the outfit made her large eyes look far more violet than blue. She had a spray of orchids pinned to the front of the dress, and their colour exactly matched the faint creamy pink of her flawless skin.

Elizabeth also wore blue, but it was rather more a delphinium blue, which lent depth to her grey eyes as well. Her flowers were half-opened palest yellow roses, and by comparison with the orchids they looked strikingly unsophisticated, just as Elizabeth herself looked completely unsophisticated at the side of the ravishing widow.

At last the toasts were over, and Nigel Van Kane had returned a polite little speech of thanks in reply to the best man's speech prophesying a completely unsullied future for himself and his bride. Then Nigel looked at his watch, and in view of the fact that they had a plane to catch he suggested breaking up the party, or that Elizabeth should at least withdraw to make whatever changes were necessary in her wearing apparel before setting out for the airstrip.

Elizabeth accepted the hint that the frivolous side of this day was over, and with Carol accompanying her she went upstairs to the room that had been specially reserved for the purpose and changed into her going-away clothes.

The change was quickly effected, for she had received the impression that Nigel was anxious, perhaps eager, to get away. And when she was ready Mrs. Wainwright examined her appearance carefully and then told her that she looked very nice indeed, in fact extremely nice.

Elizabeth was not particularly interested in the way she looked just then, although she was aware that the suit she had chosen for the occasion would have become most young women of her slenderness of build who were not downright unattractive. It was fuchsia-pink shantung, and with it she wore a little pink hat, and gloves and shoes of palest grey. When she was finally ready Mrs. Wainwright gave a quick pinch to her cheek, because she said she looked rather pale, and then suggested a light touch of rouge because it was not right for a bride to look pale when she went away to her honeymoon.

"After all, it's the only honeymoon you're likely to have, and there's no need to appear apprehensive at the outset," the older woman observed, smiling for the first time that day in the way Elizabeth did not altogether like. "You're not apprehensive, are you? You're quite happy about everything?"

"Of course," Elizabeth answered.

"And a good many women would give their eyes to have snaffled Nigel for a husband! You're lucky, you know, although you may not realise it."

Elizabeth was silent, disliking the suggestion that Nigel was the type of man who would allow himself to be "snaffled", and Mrs. Wainwright picked up her brand new handbag with the large gold clasp and put it into her hands.

"I'll tell you one thing, my dear, before we say goodbye," she said, "and offer you one bit of advice! Don't expect too much from Nigel, and don't imagine you are the only woman who has ever had any part or lot in his life! Men don't live to be thirty-five without acquiring experience, you know!"—looking at the slim form of the girl in front of her through suddenly decidedly narrowed and very brilliant blue eyes. "And in the case of Nigel, the only reason he hasn't married before this is because—"

She broke off, and Elizabeth felt her heart begin to labour suddenly and heavily inside her, and although she did not know it her own eyes betrayed the fact that all at once she was on the alert and mentally shrinking from something which she felt was about to be broken to her. Something which she knew she would not want to hear!

Carol smiled at her, and it was a smile that was just a little pitying, and just a little contemptuous.

"*I* have loved Nigel for years, and I think I can truthfully say he has loved me for the same length of time," she shattered the young bride's already precariously built-up peace of mind by confessing abruptly. "I would have married him instead of Bryn, only we quarrelled, and before we could patch it up again I allowed Bryn to over-persuade me and become Mrs. Wainwright instead of Mrs. Van Kane! It was one of those things that happen sometimes in life and about which one can do nothing – when it's too late!" There was a bitter note in her voice. "Nigel, of course, never forgave me, and now perhaps you can understand why he picked on you when he made up his mind that it was high time he did marry, and why you found it such a simple matter to get him to think seriously about you when so many others have tried to do that very thing and failed! *You* won't make demands on him – or he doesn't think you will," sneeringly, "and you're nicely brought up, and you behave yourself nicely, and he was very fond of your father! No doubt it was your father who first put it into his head!"

She opened her handbag and produced her cigarette-case and lighted herself a cigarette rather hastily. She was breathing quickly, and underneath her make-up she was almost as pale as Elizabeth, and her eyes were dark and resentful.

"In a short time you'll have developed into the kind of wife he wants – a wife who won't in the least object to being thrust into the background and kept there, and whom he can forget about it if he wishes once you've settled down into his home, although, being the type of man he is, he'll never misuse you or fail to do his duty by you. You might even be able to trust him when other women are around—"

Elizabeth cut short the tirade by speaking in a voice she did not recognise as her own.

"Have you finished?" she asked quietly.

"Not quite." Carol Wainwright was obviously fighting now for her composure, but she had a final shot in her locker. "And just in case you think you might one day be able to win him over and make an impression on him—get him to fall in love with you!—it's just as well you should know that Nigel isn't made that way. *Why* do you think he picked on my house for you to stay in, and why does he always drag me into the picture? Why do you think he and Mark Temple *loathe* one another, although on the surface remaining friends? Ask yourself these questions, and see if you can work out the answers!"

She picked up Elizabeth's light dressing-case and walked with it to the door.

"Come along now, or your husband will be getting impatient – or suspicious!" She flashed Elizabeth a look that no longer made any pretence at liking. "Have a good time while you're away," she drawled as they walked along cool corridors in the direction of the elevator. "And remember what I said about not expecting too much. In this life it's never advisable to do that!" She smiled with her exquisitely made-up lips, but not with her eyes, as the elevator shot downwards to the ground floor of the hotel.

# Chapter Thirteen

They were flying over jungle, and as Elizabeth looked downwards out of the window beside her she thought she could make out the windings of a river which from that height looked like a narrow strip of silver ribbon.

They had changed planes once. This aircraft was small and decidedly bumpy, and apart from herself and her husband there was only one other passenger. Elizabeth had done so little flying in her life – her only other air journey had been from London to Paris – that this experience could have proved alarming to her, for there was no air-hostess, no one to make certain that the frayed seat-belts were adjusted at the appropriate times, and the pilot looked young and inexperienced. However, he was quite obviously completely confident, and uninterested in anything that went on outside his own cockpit.

Very soon after taking off they ran into a storm, a violent tropical storm, and normally Elizabeth would have been petrified, especially when the lightning played over the wings, and crackled and hissed in her ears, and the tiny machine was so badly buffeted by the atmospheric conditions that it did everything but turn completely upside down in its determined attempts to maintain itself in the air.

The passenger on the other side of the cabin was violently airsick, and Nigel – who had never been either seasick or airsick in his life, and he had travelled considerably – regarded him with noticeable disgust. But Elizabeth did nothing to disgrace herself, and in fact she was so extraordinarily calm and composed that the man she had married only that morning, every time he turned his eyes upon her, betrayed the fact that he thought her performance remarkable, and deserving of high praise.

He even uttered the praise when they won clear of the storm, and it was possible to make oneself heard when one spoke. He said he was sorry she had had this kind of an experience, but it didn't often happen, and it just happened to be an unfortunate patch of bad weather. But Elizabeth seemed hardly to be aware that he was commiserating with her, or even that he obviously thought highly of her admirably controlled nerves, and she replied in a flat voice that she had not really been in the least afraid – which was true, because she no longer seemed to have very much feeling about anything – and that in any case was an experience, and an experience was always worth having.

"Is it?" Nigel looked at her with black brows concentrated in a straight line above somewhat thoughtful dark eyes. "It all depends, I would have said, upon the kind of experience," he said slowly.

Elizabeth glanced at him, and then away. There was something penetrating in his regard which seemed to reveal the fact that she was puzzling him a little, but she did not really care. After her experience after lunch – one that she would certainly not wish to repeat – when she had learned the truth about so many things, she was impervious to a good deal that would have worried her only twelve hours before.

After the storm they flew into brilliant weather again, although the sun was getting near its setting. When she stared downwards out of the window beside her now Elizabeth could see vast stretches of open veld, vividly green in the rosy, flushed light, and red ribbons of road criss-crossing it. In the distance there was something which looked like the sea, but was actually blue hills retreating into the even dimmer distance.

When at last they were coming in to land she saw a team of bright red oxen yoked two by two, drawing a wagon, and in front of the team walked a half-naked black boy who was staring upwards at the bright silvery bird that was swooping downwards from the sky. Beneath a line of blue gums some Cape carts and one or two cars were drawn up, and there were a few people standing waiting for the aircraft to disgorge its small quantity of passengers, and take on the few who wished to proceed in her.

"Welcome to Baroti!" said a hearty English voice, and a young man with face burnt to the colour of old bricks by the sun, and bleached fair hair that stood up on his head like a kind of thatch, held out an impulsive hand to Elizabeth as she was assisted to return to earth by her husband, and gazed up blankly into his face. "And heartiest congratulations, Mr. and Mrs. Van Kane!"

Nigel smiled at him rather dryly.

"Those are probably the most sincere congratulations we've received today," he observed quietly. And then he introduced the young man to Elizabeth. "This is George Baker, who runs the farm for me," he said. "Very capable, and tremendously trustworthy. Well, George, how are things?"

"Thriving," George replied. "At least," he added, with an attractive grin, "reasonably thriving." And then he looked at Elizabeth, standing very still and obviously drooping a little in her fuchsia-pink suit, with the pink hat sitting like a pink leaf on her curls. "I hope you don't mind travelling in a Land-Rover?" he asked. "It's not much more than ten miles, and I've got a couple of new tyres, so you won't feel the bumps, but I expect you've had rather an exhausting day, haven't you? I've never been married myself, but I should imagine it's the sort of thing that takes the stuffing out of you."

His breezy talk made Elizabeth, although she felt as if she had lived through a lifetime of exhausting experiences that day, lift her head up and smile at him. And when he carefully shook out a rug and placed it on the back seat of the car before she sat down, and cleared the floor space of a certain amount of impedimenta likely to do damage to her elegant new shoes, the smile became more natural, and even touched her eyes.

Nigel, however, had adopted an expression that was somewhat withdrawn, and she was not altogether surprised when he sat beside George at the wheel of the car and discussed the affairs of the farm with him while they drove.

It was not yet dark, and Elizabeth found herself peering through the protective side-screens with a certain stirring of interest as they bumped along over a very rough and uneven road. It was so rough that she found herself forced to cling to the edge of the seat at times in order to prevent herself from being flung forward on top of the other two, but this was country that in her opinion much more nearly resembled the Africa of her previous imaginings – before she had seen anything at all of it, that is – than the rich fertile country outside Cape Town and immediately surrounding Groote Kloof.

It was a bald land tufted with spears of green that rose up out of the rocky soil, and parched plants that clung to the side of little hills, or kopjes. It reminded her a bit of films she had seen of the Arizona desert, and ahead of them the brick-red road twisted and wound its way into apparently illimitable wilderness. In the last light of day there was something stark and beautiful about it that appealed to her, although the starkness vanished when they topped a rise, and there instead of continuing wilderness was a sudden stretch of green ahead of them.

They dipped down into a valley that was lined with poplar trees, lush and cool and cultivated. There were acres of neatly fenced thriving-looking crops, and dairy herds wandering at will, or so it seemed. There were one or two farmhouses wearing an air of moderate prosperity, which they passed, with the Land-Rover clinging determinedly to the persistently rough surface of the road. And then, as the sun sank slowly lower and lower, they climbed to a lonely eminence where a hushed silence lay over everything, and once again they could see the vast distance, and for miles around the bushes and clumps of succulent growth were touched like the waves of the sea, by the golden radiance of the setting sun.

The sun sank lower, ready to drop from sight behind the blue line of mountains and banners of pink and angry red flamed in the sky. Elizabeth caught sight of a small, strongly built house with a garden in front of it that reminded her vividly of a cottage garden in England. It was a riot of flowers, with a narrow path leading from the rickety garden gate to a veranda that was approached by a couple of low steps, and there were chairs and tables in the veranda looking out towards the setting sun.

George Baker brought the car to rest outside the garden gate, and then he sprang down and held open the rear door for Elizabeth, who alighted more slowly, feeling stiff after her hours of travelling. She stared at the front of the house, which was apparently another property belonging to her husband, and the thought in her mind as her eyes rested on the unpretentious but homely-looking small dwelling was that here, if one was on a strictly normal honeymoon, was the ideal honeymoon house!

Nigel Van Kane left George to deal with the assortment of luggage and came up quietly behind his newly made wife and looked at her in a way that she found difficult to analyse. There was nothing in her eyes that she recognised – neither mockery, nor friendliness, nor even questioning. They simply seemed to her blank and watchful and waiting.

"Well, what do you think of it?" he asked. "It's a bit primitive, isn't it, after Groote Kloof, but I always like being here."

"Do you?" she said. She looked about her rather vaguely, thinking that in another two minutes the dark would have descended, and the whole place would be walled in by the mystery of the night. "It's lonely, isn't it?"

"Too lonely." This time she knew that his voice was mocking.

"Not for me." But she could not prevent herself from sounding stiff and detached. Since lunch she felt that tremendous gulf had opened up between them, and it was a gulf that would go on widening because neither he nor she had the power to bridge it. It was a gulf that made her feel sick and cold inside, and she wondered whether he was aware of it, too, or whether he was still in ignorance that such a chasm had resulted from a few minutes in a hotel bedroom with the woman he had once loved, and almost certainly still did.

She looked up at him in the warm and sensuous dusk that was closing round them, aware that stars were already pricking like green fire the haze above their heads, and her face was suddenly white and weary. With a gesture of insupportable weariness and impatience she removed the flippant little hat from her head and her flattened gold curls, and stood holding it in her hands.

"I'm not afraid of loneliness," she said, very distinctly, and then left him and went up the path in the wake of George and their suitcases, and watched the latter handing them over to a widely grinning and very youthful black servant who had abruptly appeared from nowhere, while a light sprang up in the living room of the house.

# Chapter Fourteen

Jackson, as the black servant called himself, showed Elizabeth to her room, and then stood waiting with a rather anxious expression on his face while she looked round it.

It was a reasonably large room, with the bare minimum of furniture, but everything inside it was spotlessly clean and fresh, and the floor and the furniture shone as if they had been recently polished with gusto. There were even a few flowers in a vase on the dressing-table; Elizabeth noticed them at once, and in ordinary circumstances she would have let Jackson know immediately how much she appreciated this rather touching evidence of his desire to accord her some sort of welcome. But tonight she was too keenly aware of that spreading sea of unhappiness and disillusion inside her to be capable of remembering what was expected of her.

She could only sink down rather limply into a creaking basket chair and smile at him rather wanly.

The first thing she had noticed about the room was that there were two beds in it – two unostentatious single beds with woven counterpanes which matched the curtains. She was still sitting staring as if hypnotised by the sight of that other bed when Nigel made his appearance in the doorway of the room and stood looking in at her with an expression of sharpness on his face.

"George is just leaving," he said, "and I've asked him to have a drink. Will you come and join us?"

His voice was cold and frigidly formal, and Elizabeth looked up almost guiltily.

"Of course. I—I didn't realise he didn't live here. Of course I'll come."

"George is rather old-fashioned, and he believes that two's company and three's none," her husband explained in acid accents. "He does live here normally, but while we're here he's taking up his quarters in a bungalow about a mile farther on, which was the original living quarters of the farm."

"I see," Elizabeth said. She met his eyes for a moment, feeling that they were the eyes of a complete stranger, and then stood up.

She followed him into the combined living room and dining room, where the oil lamp was sending out golden rays across the furniture. It was a room where the equipment had been well thought out in a way that would be highly satisfactory to a bachelor, and here again there were flowers – little tight clusters of them crammed into every available container that would hold them. It was a little ironical that Jackson, who was a Mission School product, had recognised the symbolism of white in connection with a bride, and most of the flowers were white, and for the most part they gave off a heavy and rather sickly scent.

George was standing in the middle of the room with a glass of sherry in his hand, and he was looking uncomfortable and rather embarrassed, Elizabeth thought. He grinned at her when she made her appearance in the wake of Nigel, still wearing her slightly crumpled pink suit, and with her fair hair still lying flattened to her head after the pressure it had received from the hat she had worn all day.

"You shouldn't have bothered to come back to say goodbye to me, Mrs. Van Kane," he told her. "You'll be seeing more of me, and in any case you must be pretty well all in after such a hectic day." From the revealing tiredness of her face she was decidedly "all in", and he looked at her sympathetically, but with a certain puzzlement in his eyes. "Was today the first time you have flown anywhere in Africa?"

"Yes." Elizabeth had a glass of sherry put into her hand by her husband, and she took a quick sip at it. "And we ran into a storm. It was my first experience of a tropical storm."

"But nevertheless you came through it with flying colours," Nigel observed rather dryly.

"Splendid!" George exclaimed, and then set down his glass on an occasional table near to him. He declined to have another drink when pressed. "Remember, I've got to drive another mile!" His grin was infectious. "And besides, I hate inflicting myself like this on you two lovebirds …!"

Elizabeth's face remained pale and unsmiling, and her husband's took on a slightly cynical expression.

When he was gone, and they could hear his car roaring away down the bumpy road, Van Kane poured himself another drink and tossed it off rather hastily, and then he turned to Elizabeth.

"If I were you," he said, "I wouldn't bother very much about unpacking tonight. But I'd get Jackson to run you a hot bath, and then we'll have dinner if you feel like it. I noticed that you didn't make a particularly hearty lunch," studying the depressed outline of her young, wan-looking face, and the mauve smudges beneath the heavy eyes that might have been due to nothing more than physical weariness, especially as her mouth drooped with weariness, too. "I'm afraid it has been rather a day for you."

She lifted her eyes to his face, and then dropped them again almost instantly.

"I'll survive it," she answered briefly, and then turned away.

The bath Jackson prepared for her was really hot, and although the bathroom itself was primitive she enjoyed the half-hour devoted to restoring some kind of animation to her heavy-feeling limbs. And when she returned to her bedroom and put on a new white dress patterned with sprigs of little blue flowers, she even felt capable of regarding her reflection in the mirror without being revolted by the evidence of an overwhelming pallor.

She had locked the bedroom door on returning to it from the bathroom, but there was no sign that in her absence any additional luggage had been deposited in the room, and only her own suitcases and her large cabin trunk were waiting to be unpacked.

She felt so relieved by what now struck her as proof that despite her changed status she was to have the room to herself, that the colour she had been tempted to apply to her cheeks out of a pot now flooded into them in a most natural manner, and she felt able to breathe more easily. And when she returned to the living room the sight of Nigel, beautifully shaved and ready for the evening, waiting for her in front of the rather crude brick hearth, was additional confirmation that he had a bedroom of his own, and that his toilet had been performed there while she was taking time over performing her own.

Nigel's eyes flickered up at her, and he took in all the details of the white dress. And he saw that she was now looking far more like herself, although still unwilling to meet his glance for more than a moment, and with a noticeable air of stiffness and restraint about her manner.

Jackson served them with a really excellently cooked and prepared meal, and even Elizabeth felt as if new life was flowing back into her after the iced fruit cocktail, the tender chicken garnished with mushrooms and accompanied by peas that she was quite certain were not tinned, and the wonderful concoction made up of ice cream, nuts, and slices of pawpaw and raisins that rounded off the meal.

Coffee was served to them on the veranda, and it was when the mellow light of the living room was behind them and they were out there lying in long cane chairs – or rather, Elizabeth was sitting rather uncomfortably upright in hers – that the feeling of tension began again, and her intense awareness of the man sharing the veranda with her began to affect Elizabeth with nervousness because she was so certain that he must be able to sense the chaotic condition into which her mind was flung because they were at last alone together as husband and wife.

The moon was rising. It was climbing very slowly into the sky, and as it rose a silver haze spread over all the surrounding country. Each bush and shrub stood out, ambushed by shadow, and bats went flickering under the eaves of the house, making queer little whistling noises as they flew by. Apart from that the silence in which this new, strange land was locked impressed Elizabeth as nothing she had experienced since her arrival in Africa had impressed her, for it was a silence that filled her with an acute realisation of their loneliness, and the primitive conditions that were not far away from her.

And yet there was also a kind of primitive peace in this silence and this isolation, if only one could relax. But Elizabeth, clasping her hands tightly together in her lap, knew that she was quite unable to relax just then.

Her husband, ignoring his coffee, was lying back in his chair and staring out into the shadows that surrounded them on three sides — or he appeared to be staring into the shadows every time her own eyes fluttered towards him. And, so far as she could judge, he was quite relaxed. His hand lay resting on the arm of his chair, a cigarette between the long, firm fingers, and a spiral of smoke curled upwards between them as the cigarette burned away slowly. He was apparently unaware of it, so removed were his thoughts, and so complete his mood of calm and sustained detachment.

Elizabeth felt envious of that mood of his, and at the same time resented it as she had probably never resented anything before in her life, because it told her so plainly how far from her his thoughts could travel, even on their wedding night, and how little the ceremony of that morning meant to him.

Carol Wainwright had invented nothing when she had robbed her of all her hopes before she left Cape Town. The reason why she was now a married woman was not because the man she had married had wanted to marry her – he had married her because he had thought it a good idea, and he had known it would please her father. So far as he himself was concerned he had loved one woman once, and he was not prepared to love any other woman again. Certainly not Elizabeth, who was too young and inexperienced, but would probably make him a good and undemanding wife!

Elizabeth made a little, unconscious movement of protest as she thought these thoughts, and instantly the man opposite her cast aside his abstraction and became aware of her.

"You're tired?" he said, throwing away his burnt-out cigarette with a movement of disgust. "You'd like to go to bed?"

"I—y—yes—n—no—" Elizabeth was all at once so nervous that she found she could not altogether control her speech, and she was afraid that the tremor in her voice must strike him as extraordinary. For why should she be so nervous when there was absolutely nothing in his manner to make her so, when for the past ten minutes he had been so unaware of her that he had even forgotten her existence temporarily? She was quite sure of that. And she was sure now that the look he sent in her direction was made up of a certain amount of amazement, faint curiosity, and perhaps just the merest blend of humour.

"I think it would be quite a good idea if you went to bed early," he said, "because you've had quite a long day. And getting married – as George remarked," with a curious twist to his lips, "can be exhausting, especially when you're not used to it!"

Elizabeth stood up suddenly, and all at once, she was conscious of so much frustration, and so much indignation and hurt, that she was quite powerless to prevent some of it being given away by her shaking voice and her pale-faced mutinous look as she turned on him and gripped the veranda rail.

"If you want me to go to bed you have only to tell me so," she said. "I'm not a child to be ordered to bed, or to have its advantages recommended to me!"

Her voice was shaking so much now that it was almost pitiful, and her hand that was gripping the veranda post was shaking also. "I expect you'd like to be left alone to think about Carol, wouldn't you? And how very different you would be feeling tonight if, instead of acquiring me for a bride, you had found it possible to forgive her defection and married her instead! As you ought to have done, as she has been expecting you to do ever since her husband died!"

The spate of words dried up suddenly as if the furious passage she had given to them had burnt her throat, and it was no longer capable of making any utterance. But the man who had listened with absolutely no expression on his face, and who was now standing up and quietly facing her, said nothing at all, and as she dared not look at his face – and, in any case, it revealed nothing – she had no idea what he was thinking, or how he was affected by her verbal bombshell, which must have been quite unlooked for.

She turned gropingly towards the glass doors behind them, and started to push them open, but he still said nothing. The door stuck in her hand and she had to give it a push, and she was still pushing and trembling and ready to burst into tears when he said, "Wait!"

But nothing would have induced her to wait then, and she took a few quick steps across the floor of the lounge. She called over her shoulder: "I'm going to take your advice and go to bed! Goodnight!"

And before he could say "Wait!" again, she had the door of her bedroom opened, had slipped inside and shut it and he heard the key rasp noisily in the lock.

# Chapter Fifteen

Elizabeth stood leaning against the door for several seconds after she had shut it and locked it, and her heart beat so wildly that she thought it would choke her. The house was very silent and still, and she could detect no movement on the other side of the door. Nigel, if he had followed her to her own room, must have withdrawn again to the veranda, and was probably thinking over her outburst while reclining again in his long chair. No doubt he was a little perturbed, because a wife who indulged in hysterical accusations on her wedding night was hardly the sort of wife he would have chosen if he had been aware of her potentialities beforehand.

Elizabeth, however, was not altogether sorry for what she had said. It had had to be said, and the fact that she had let it escape her tonight did not entirely dismay her. The only thing that did dismay her was that, the truth having been laid bare between them, nothing and no one could alter the situation that had now arisen, and which must inevitably affect their relations in the future.

She knew now why he had married her, and he knew that she knew about Carol. Carol would always be a barrier between them, and because of her they could never even get back to their old friendly footing.

Not that he ever pretended to love her! He had never even told her that he liked her very much! And he had only kissed her on one occasion, the merest butterfly caress to give her reassurance – and that, although it seemed impossible to her now, was the night before.

Still shaking in every limb, she moved away from the door and switched on the bedside lamp, which stood on a table placed midway between the two narrow beds. She sat down on one of the beds and wrapped her arms tightly about her knees in order to steady their trembling, but her tongue felt dry and refused to be moistened, and she was a little frightened. She felt lonely and cut off and conscious of having made an appalling mistake which could hardly now be remedied, although surely something would have to be done to remedy it?

Bathed in the mellow glow from the lamp, which turned her bridal white to a faint rosy pink, she sat staring at the opposite bed and subconsciously noted that its woven counterpane had been removed, that the sheets were turned down and that it was ready for an occupant, just as the bed on which she was seated was ready for an occupant.

Jackson's idea she wondered? He could surely not be acting on instructions!

There came a sudden sharp rap at the door, and she sat up stiffly.

"Open the door, Elizabeth!" her husband's voice commanded quietly. "I want to talk to you."

Elizabeth made no reply, but her heart started to labour heavily again.

"Elizabeth!" Nigel commanded sharply. "You're not in bed, are you? So please open the door!"

"Why?" Her voice was a little more controlled than it had been, but it was low and barely reached him.

He shook the door handle impatiently.

"I want to talk to you, Elizabeth! If you've started to undress, put on a dressing-gown and come out into the lounge."

Elizabeth rose then and moved with dignity towards the door. With fingers that were much less inclined to fumble than they had been she turned the key and opened the door quietly, and when she saw him standing there facing her she did not lower her eyes. The soft light behind her made her, in her pale dress, look fragile and defenceless, but in spite of the emotional disturbance that had shaken her so recently her expression was calm as she walked into the lounge.

All the lights were blazing away there, and the door to the veranda was closed. As she looked round the room and Nigel, behind her, closed the door to her bedroom, she knew, for a moment, an absurd sensation like being trapped and shut in with him, but nothing of this showed in her face as she stood in front of the fireplace and faced him.

"What do you want to talk to me about?"

He drew forward a chair and indicated it.

"Sit down," he said.

Elizabeth sat down obediently. His attitude was very quiet and controlled, but she did not altogether like the iron rigidity of his face. His eyes, when he offered her a cigarette, were not the eyes of the man she had known, not even in the earliest days of their acquaintance. They seemed to have narrowed, for one thing, and they lent a mask-like look to his face. And underneath the thick eyelashes there was nothing but a cold gleam.

"Would you like something to drink?" he inquired politely. "To settle your nerves," he added, in the driest of tones.

"No, thank you," Elizabeth answered.

"You're quite sure?"

"Quite."

The crispness of her tone this time caused him to study her for a few moments very deliberately, and then he started to speak, taking up his own position in front of the fireplace, while the scent of the waxen white flowers floated heavily in the room, and Elizabeth began to wish that he had not closed the door to the veranda, for the night was very warm, and there was not enough cool air churned up by the electric fans.

"Would you mind repeating to me what you said out there on the veranda before you so hurriedly departed to your room?" the man's emotionless voice demanded quietly. "It is just possible, I realise, that I didn't hear you aright, but somehow I think I did! You were implying—or perhaps you did more than imply?—that Mrs.

Wainwright and myself were much more than old friends. Lovers, in fact!"

Elizabeth's voice sounded suddenly stifled again as she answered: "Well, and can you deny it? Would you even attempt to deny it?"

"I might." He was leaning back against the rough edge of the brick mantelpiece behind him, and there was something almost insolent in the way he lounged there, she thought. Insolent and contemptuous at the same time. "I might, but on the other hand I might not. It all depends upon whether or not you would believe me. I am inclined to suppose that you would not."

Elizabeth clenched her hands together so tightly in her lap that the nails dug into the soft flesh.

"Why did you marry me?" she asked, and she had to make a tremendous effort to keep the words steady.

For an instant something like the reflection of a smile she had seen on his face more than once before appeared in his eyes, lightening their expression in a way that was almost a relief, and his lips curved upwards for a moment. And then the reflected glimmer of a smile was gone, and he was confronting her as if all at once they had become the bitterest enemies.

"Shall I say because your father thought it was a good plan?" he returned with silken smoothness.

She bit her lip.

"And for no other reason?"

"What other reason could there be?"

Elizabeth felt she could sit still no longer and listen to him making replies that reduced her to the level of an inanimate object, and if he was angry she became suddenly angrier, and she stood up and faced him with nothing more than a bare foot of space between them, while her slender bosom heaved and her eyes flashed sparks.

"I think you knew very well that Mrs. Wainwright told me the truth before we left Cape Town," she said, "but I don't suppose you realise how much I feel indebted to her because she did tell me the truth – because she opened my eyes for me!"

"On the contrary," he assured her, throwing away the end of his cigarette and lighting another, "I have no doubt at all that Mrs.

Wainwright told you the truth so convincingly that it would be astonishing if your eyes had not been opened! But the one thing Mrs. Wainwright could not accuse me of was deliberately misleading you. I asked you to marry me, and you accepted! Did I ever tell you that I had never loved any woman before in my life, and in point of fact did I ever mention love to you at all?"

"N—no," she stammered.

"And you were content to marry me without a protestation of any sort of devotion, or without apparently caring for me in the slightest degree yourself, simply because your father approved, and because, on thinking the matter over, you decided that there were advantages in becoming my wife which were greater than going home to England and taking up the threads of your old existence there, which no doubt had proved a trifle boring." His voice stung like a whiplash now, and she could sense that his indignation was so great that instead of boiling up into a kind of white-hot fury inside him it was transmuting him into a kind of pillar of ice that would forgive her nothing, hear nothing in her favour. "You came out to Africa to visit your father and have a good time. Unfortunately that good time failed, and my proposal was something that you snatched at because it made it unnecessary for you ever to think about going back to England and that life you were quite happy to forget all about! If you can deny that, you can also deny that it never apparently disturbed you in the least that my proposal was so unromantic, and that it included none of the promises and the protestations normal proposals do carry with them!"

Elizabeth gasped before this decided attack, but everything he said was so true – apart from the fact that she had *not* come out to visit her father just to have a good time – that her mental equipment refused to aid her for a few moments, and she could not think how to answer him, or how to deny the accusations. And he went on, scathingly: "And more than that, having agreed without any sort of a demur to the arrangement I suggested, and found no fault with it whatsoever, you allow yourself to be upset on your wedding day because a woman tells you I was once in love with her—and she was not, if you would care to know it, telling you any lies!—and start treating me as if I was something that had suddenly acquired the label 'untouchable' even before we had properly started out on our honeymoon journey! I knew from the moment you reappeared in the dining room at the hotel after being closeted upstairs too long with Carol that everything was far from being as it had been in the morning between us, and in the plane when the storm was on you were so full of your sense of injury that you found it impossible to be frightened. That's true, isn't it?"

He suddenly strode to the veranda door and flung it wide open as if feeling the need for air, and then he turned back to her and looked at her across the width of the brightly lighted room, and his face looked both pale and implacable.

"Well?" he demanded harshly. "Where do we go from here? What do you want me to do about things now? Set the machinery in motion for an annulment of our marriage?"

This was carrying the attack with so much vigour into her own camp that Elizabeth could only gasp at him for a moment as if he had actually hit her across the face. She felt as if a weapon that she had thought securely clasped in her own hand had been most unexpectedly wrenched away from her, and was now being wielded with considerable effect against herself.

She swallowed, and her eyes grew black and bewildered.

"Well?" he insisted, mockingly waiting for her answer. Elizabeth made an attempt to vindicate herself and her actions before he crushed her completely.

"I don't know what you are talking about," she told him, "but it's not true that I—that I—"

"That you married me for, shall we say, security, and a share of my material assets?" His smile made her blush hotly, because it was so openly full of cynicism.

"Of course it's not true! I mean—" she stammered, "I married you because—"

"Because it seemed like an excellent arrangement?"

"We—we both thought it was a good arrangement—"

"But we neither of us are so strongly inclined to view it from that angle tonight!" His smile had vanished, and his voice was like ice again. "You'd better go to bed. We've talked round this thing enough for one night, and going on talking won't clarify the position for either of us. Besides, you probably want some sleep, and I know I do."

He went to the door of her bedroom and held it open for her, and she realised that she was being dismissed. She looked at him for a moment with almost a hint of appeal in her eyes, but he either didn't recognise it or didn't see it. She wanted to tell him that although he was quite right when he said she had married him because she thought it was a good arrangement, it was not only because of that – and but for the fact that he had come to mean so much in her life that she literally hadn't the power to refuse him when he asked her, she would have refused him. The idea of an "arrangement" had repelled her from the first. But it was like half a loaf being better than no bread! She had *had* to possess the half loaf!

But how could she tell him that? Even if he had not so recently torn her to pieces with words that she would never forget, it was impossible for her ever to disclose to him the real reason why she had married him.

It would be too utterly humiliating, now that she knew the truth about him. For he had just admitted that Carol had told her nothing but the truth!

She turned and walked blindly through the open doorway into her cheerfully lighted room, and she did not even answer when he said good night to her coldly.

Just before she heard him close the door behind her she also heard his cutting recommendation: "You can lock your door if you like, but it really isn't necessary. You're quite safe!"

# Chapter Sixteen

Elizabeth felt as if sleep was the last thing that would ever come upon her as she lay in the deep, suffocating darkness of her room with the door unlocked – somehow she had found it impossible to turn the key in the lock after Nigel had sarcastically informed her that it was unnecessary for her to do so – and the realisation that he was sleeping not very far away from her was enough to keep her even more wakeful.

As she tossed and turned in the darkness she couldn't help wondering how this day would have ended if she had never had that brief period of enlightenment forced upon her by Carol. Only last night, when he said good night to her, the man who was now her husband had kissed her for the first time since their engagement, and he had surprised her with the kiss – surprised her because of something she had glimpsed, or thought she glimpsed, in his eyes, just before his lips lightly brushed her forehead.

But whatever that something was she was never likely to see it again in his eyes, and it was quite probable that she had imagined it — in fact, more than probable!

So far as she could think clearly at the moment, there was only one course open to her. Nigel had said that discussing the matter would lead them nowhere, and he was right. He was right in so much that he had said that the very memory of his words stung her like actual scourges, and she crouched down amongst her pillows with a sensation of burning shame crowding upon her because he had been so right.

She had not even bothered to find out what he really thought of her before saying "yes" to his suggestion of marriage! She had not even asked for time to think it over, or taken a day to think it over – she had accepted him at once!

So naturally he had decided that it was the "arrangement" that had appealed to her. And having agreed to an "arrangement" she had no right to expect anything more from him.

But there was one thing she could do, before it was too late. He had mentioned annulment. The marriage would have to be annulled! She would go away as soon as possible—tomorrow, if only she could manage it!—and leave the field clear for him to do whatever he liked. She had no doubt at all that he would take the wisest step and rid himself of her without any delay. It would be the only sensible step he could take …

And as for her … She was not at all sure what she would do, or how she would get through the rest of her life, but it didn't really matter in any case. Nothing mattered any more. Only Nigel would be free again, and once free he would surely see the wisdom of patching up his quarrel with the woman he still loved, forgetting his pride, and do the thing she wanted him to do more than anything else. Marry her …!

And Elizabeth would go home to England, she supposed, and somehow she would take up the threads of her existence in England again, and if her mother and sisters proved curious she would just tell them that she had made a mistake. Which was exactly what she had done!

She managed to get to sleep at last, and in the morning Jackson brought her her early tea, and then she took a bath and dressed herself and made her way somewhat apprehensively into the living room. But although breakfast was laid for her there, Nigel had already had his, and his seat at the table was empty.

After breakfast she waited for him to appear, but as he did not do so she questioned Jackson and he told her, with his broad smile, that the "baas" would not be back until lunch time. From which Elizabeth gathered that the master of the place was making the rounds of his farm, probably in the company of George Baker.

She was half fearful that George would return with him for lunch, and when he did not do so she realised how much she had been spared. For to have had to put up a pretence of normal composure under the circumstances would have been difficult enough, but to have had to pretend in addition that she was a newly wedded wife blissfully in love with her husband would have been well-nigh impossible.

But when Nigel returned he returned alone, and he greeted Elizabeth in much the same manner as he had been accustomed to greet her when she had stayed as a guest at his house in the first few days after her arrival in Africa. There was a cool smile in his eyes in addition to something slightly disdainful, and a brittle politeness in his voice when he addressed her.

She was sitting alone on the veranda when he appeared suddenly from behind the house, and although she looked rather a small and forlorn figure she obviously did not strike him that way. He called Jackson and instructed him to bring drinks, and while they waited for the service of lunch to commence he talked in a detached voice about affairs at the farm, and appeared to be completely absorbed and wrapped up in nothing else.

Elizabeth, who had been dreading this moment when she would come face to face with him again after last night, was yet conscious of a curious, searing disappointment because of his utter and obvious indifference to her either as a wife or as someone who in future might be expected to run his various households for him, in return for the security which a solidly placed husband would provide her with.

After lunch he went off again, and he did not even bother to enquire how she proposed spending the afternoon. In the evening they dined together, sat for a while on the veranda while the African moon spilled its magic all about them once more, and then went to bed without either of them uttering a word that had any direct or indirect bearing on the stormy scene which had marred their wedding night.

But the following day George Baker was brought home to lunch. In the course of the lunch time conversation Elizabeth learned that he was taking the Land-Rover into Baroti the following morning, and that he would be calling at the house to pick up a parcel for delivery there on his way from his own bungalow. Nigel explained that as he probably would not be around at the time Jackson would hand over the parcel, and it was then that the idea occurred to Elizabeth which caused her to lie awake again for most of that night. When the morning came she had not shifted from her resolution.

George Baker was a simple, honest, and unassuming young man. She had already decided that. And she had decided also that he was shrewd enough to have detected almost from the beginning that all was not exactly as it should be between two newly-married people, and every time she caught his puzzled eyes lingering on her face, and then passing on to the face of her husband, she knew that he was asking himself: "Why?"

When he drove up outside the rickety garden gate about midway through the morning and saw her sitting alone on the veranda – although he did not know it, waiting for him impatiently – he leapt out of the car and smiled at her. Somewhat to *his* surprise it was she who presented him with the parcel when he went up the veranda steps. He had of course been prepared for the absence of her husband, but he was astonished when she asked him in somewhat hurried tones whether he would give her a lift into Baroti.

And then, for the first time, he noticed that she was wearing a crisp-looking new suit, and her hat was sitting waiting for her on a chair, and so was a small kind of weekend case.

"A lift into Baroti?" His sandy eyebrows raised themselves. "But what for?"

Elizabeth decided that there was no point at all in dissembling.

"Because I want to catch the plane which arrives there this afternoon!" she said simply. "The plane which goes on to Cape Town, or at least a part of the way. I believe I have to transfer to another aircraft before the journey is completed, but the important thing is that I must catch the plane at Baroti!"

George, although she was still standing, sat down rather suddenly on a basket chair in front of her.

"But you can't—you can't do a thing like that!" he said. "What on earth would Nigel have to say?"

Elizabeth decided to be even more straightforward and truthful.

"It doesn't matter what he says or thinks," she told him. Her face looked grave and small and disillusioned – rather wearily disillusioned – in the deep, cool shade of the veranda. "And as he won't be asked about my going, he's not likely to say anything – at any rate, until I'm gone!"

"You mean—?" George's mouth gaped open, rather like that of a fish.

"That I'm running away! At least, I'm going back to Cape Town, and when I get to Cape Town I shall go home to England in the first ship that can provide me with a passage, or I may even fly home if I can afford the fare. But I'm going." Her softly lovely mouth set in lines of determination. "If you won't take me to Baroti, Mr. Baker, I shall have to find some other means of getting there, but you can take it that I'm quite serious about going. I've *got* to go!"

"Why?" George closed his mouth at last, and then he looked at her more carefully. "Don't tell me this marriage isn't turning out a success? You can't be regretting it already, because for one thing you haven't given it much of a trial, have you?"

"It never needed a trial," Elizabeth surprised him by stating emphatically. "It was just a mistake!"

George whistled.

"I must say, I didn't think you looked like the radiant bride the night you arrived," he confessed, "and, if it comes to that, Nigel wasn't appearing exactly to advantage, either. Neither of you was looking particularly perky, but I put it down to your having had a tiring day. I know these things get you down—"

"Mr. Baker," she interrupted him, "*will* you take me to Baroti?" Her fingers were closing and unclosing themselves on the handle of her bag, and for the first time he noticed the strain in her eyes, and realised that she was like a piece of tightly stretched wire that might snap at any moment if nothing was done about it. Even her voice had a nervous quiver in it — a faintly hysterical quiver, he thought. "Because if you won't—"

"Don't tell me you'll walk there," he said, gently, "because that's a physical impossibility. For you, at any rate."

"Then I'll get there somehow—"

He stood up abruptly.

"What'll I say to Nigel when I get back and he asks me if I know where you are? Do I just tell him the truth?"

"Yes. He's got to know, and it won't make any difference. Believe me it won't," urgently. "He won't come after me, I know that."

"Won't he?"

George surveyed her with a look in his eyes that baffled her, and then compassion banished that look. He bent and picked up her weekend case.

"All right! Hop into the car," he said. "But don't blame me if we run into Nigel and he orders you out again! We *are* liable to run into him at any moment, you know – at least, until we've won well clear of this place."

"I'm willing to take the risk, if you are."

"Okay!" he answered, and Elizabeth, when he climbed into the Land-Rover beside her and they started off, concentrated fiercely on the one thought in her mind — whatever happened they must *not* run into Nigel!

As luck would have it they didn't run into her husband, and they reached Baroti in record time. Elizabeth, when she caught sight of the line of blue gums beneath which the line of Cape carts and cars had waited on the evening of her arrival, felt a sudden sensation of sickness attack her inside, and the realisation that she was deliberately putting hundreds of miles between herself and Nigel struck her with force.

George helped her out of the car, and he thought he saw signs of weakening in her face.

"Changed your mind?" he suggested, still gently. "Because if you have I'll run you back—"

But Elizabeth shook her head mutely.

"Very well," he said. He looked at her for a moment and then he said: "You'd better hop back into the car, I think, while I go and make a few enquiries. We're a bit early for the regular service, but it's just possible there's another one on the run. Anyway, I'll find out if you'll stay here."

Elizabeth thanked him, and while he was absent she sat rigidly beside the untended wheel of the Land-Rover, with her hands locked tightly together in her lap, and the fierce afternoon sunlight beating down on her head and making her senses swim. When George returned she looked quite alarmingly pale from a combination of heat and inward turmoil, and he put her out of a certain amount of anxiety straight away by stating at once that she was fortunate, and a plane was due in another ten minutes that would take her the best part of the way back to Cape Town.

George helped her out of the car again, and they went and took up their positions in the shelter of the blue gums. Elizabeth gasped with relief because the atmosphere was so much cooler here, and it enabled her to think more clearly. She looked about her at the hot, dusty airstrip, and for the first time it struck her what a boon aviation must be to isolated farmers like George who lived and worked in this remote corner of Africa, and whose means of communication with the outside world it was – even though it involved risking life and limb in one of those tiny, toy-like aeroplanes such as the one she was waiting for now.

An ox-wagon came along the road – the brick-red road which led back to Nigel – and it might have been the very ox-wagon she had observed on the night she flew into Baroti. There was a chirpy, half-clad, and very small, intensely black boy walking ahead of the team, and he, too, could have been the same boy that she had seen before.

Elizabeth caught her lower lip between her teeth and bit it hard. One day in the distant future, when she got back to her own homeland, she would call up the picture of this remote, dusty, blazingly hot airstrip, with the cobalt-blue sky above it, and although it would be only a mental picture she would hardly bear to be able to look at it.

George glanced at her sideways, and at a guess he would have said that her endurance was giving out. He found her a fallen tree trunk to sit down upon, and when she did so he offered her a cigarette.

And then he sighed suddenly.

"It's a pity about Nigel and you," he observed, "a great pity. But sometimes these things do work themselves out."

Elizabeth volunteered no answer.

"And it took Nigel so many years to make up his mind about a wife that it seems a bit hard ..." He shook his head, as if deploring the whole matter. "As a matter of fact," he confessed, "we none of us thought he would ever marry, because he always said his standards were too high, and he didn't imagine he would ever meet anyone who would measure up to them. There's never been any rumour of his marrying before."

Elizabeth found herself lifting her head and studying him rather sharply.

"Not—not Mrs. Wainwright?" she said. "I understood they were engaged to be married at one time – or as good as engaged to be married!"

George appeared surprised.

"If they were, I never heard of it, and Carol Wainwright's been in and out of love with so many men at different times that I can hardly accept it that Nigel ..." He broke off and shook his head. "Extremely unlikely, I should say! He might have admired her in her extreme youth, when she wasn't quite so hardbitten, but she drove one husband to look upon suicide as a good way out, and now she's got Mark Temple lined up – but maybe he'll prove too wary and escape her yet! Nigel was telling me only a few months ago that if he was weak enough to give way he'd be deserving of all the pity that could be lavished on him, and I quite agree. Oh, no," shaking his head afresh, "I'm quite sure you've got it wrong about Nigel and Carol. She's just one of those lovely ladies who go about discarding and earmarking fresh husbands, and Nigel is the last man on earth who would fall for a woman like that – or, if he did, he'd get over it pretty quickly!"

"You think so?" Elizabeth heard herself asking him huskily.

"Dead certain of it!"

They both caught sight of a tiny silver speck approaching them high up in that brazen blue sky, and although Elizabeth would have welcomed the sight of it only a bare few moments before, she now felt completely dismayed because it was in the sky at all. And the thought that she soon would be a passenger, being borne across that wide arc herself, dismayed her still more.

"Please," she said quickly, moistening her lips, "what was it you said about Nigel and—and his high standards? The—the high standards he set for a wife?"

George smiled down at her, thinking that at last he was seeing daylight.

"Only that he would never have married you if he hadn't thought you were just the right type for him – and I'm amazed that you're going off like this because I could have sworn that you were just the right type, too!"

Elizabeth said nothing, perhaps because in that moment she did not know what to say. And considerably to her astonishment, when the plane landed at last, instead of urging her afresh to change her mind and return as he felt she ought to do to her legal lord and master, George began to appear anxious to get her off his hands and inside the aircraft, and even if she had wanted to change her mind in those last moments no opportunity was provided for her to do so.

Instead, George saw her into the cabin of the aircraft, waved her a casual farewell, turned his attention to the pilot and exchanged some lively badinage with him for about five minutes, and then went away back to where he had left the Land-Rover.

As the aeroplane rose into the blue, Elizabeth, peering wistfully downwards, saw the sturdy vehicle in which she had so recently travelled over that vivid ribbon of red road which led back to Nigel and the life that would now never be hers, returning by the way it had come. And as the watched the tiny car crawling like a fly along the road a mist rose up before her eyes and she was prevented from seeing anything clearly.

# Chapter Seventeen

Once again Elizabeth was flying over Africa, and once again, as she looked downwards, she saw the pattern of it unfolding like a giant backcloth far, far below her. There were the patches of jungle and the rivers, the sun-baked open country, the game reserves, and the mountains that enclosed the plains. As they continued in a southerly course the pattern of it hardly altered, and Elizabeth knew that there would be little change until they came almost within sight of the sea, and the rich fruit-growing country which had provided her with her first taste of Africa.

But before they were anywhere near the sea it would be necessary for her to exchange this tiny, primitive type of aircraft for one of the larger air liners belonging to the South African Airways Corporation. In the meantime, in spite of perfect flying weather, the flight was by no means as smooth as it might have been. They continually lost height and then managed to regain it, and more than once Elizabeth thought she detected an odd, uncertain note about the rhythm of the engine which could, of course, have been entirely due to her imagination-although her imagination was scarcely working overtime just then, and she was sunk in a worse kind of apathy and mental lethargy than she had been even on the flight which had followed her marriage to Nigel.

In addition she was feeling entirely hopeless, and without any sort of interest in anything that was going on around her. She could see no promise for the future, and the present was something she had to live through, but of which she was only vaguely conscious. So that when the erratic movements of the aircraft first attracted her notice they must have been going on for some considerable while and that false note in the rhythm of the engine was becoming positively jarring.

Elizabeth looked around her at the other passengers in the tiny, enclosed cabin space. There were three of them, and one was a woman not much older than herself who was travelling with a very young baby. Elizabeth felt suddenly acutely for her because she looked both tired and anxious, and the baby was exceedingly fretful. Both the other passengers were men; they were the stolid type who were accustomed to making journeys by air under these far from ideal conditions, and at the moment when Elizabeth looked round at them the faces of both were beginning to wear a somewhat critical expression. Even while she studied them the critical expressions gave way to the first faint tinge of apprehension, and as the aircraft gave a sudden, wild lurch and seemed about to catapult right down into the middle of a spreading sea of jungle below them, the apprehension quickly increased.

Elizabeth looked to see what the pilot was doing, and as she was the one who was nearest to him, and there was nothing between her and his back (which revealed great concentration) but the back of his own seat, she was able to see quite clearly the assortment of dials and levers in front of him which told her nothing at all, but which appeared to be engaging his rather desperate attention.

Suddenly he looked round over his shoulder and said shortly: "We've got to make a forced landing, but there's no need for anyone to panic. There may be a bit of a jolt, but I'll try and make it as smooth as possible. Fasten your seat-belts, please, and wait for it!"

The young woman with the baby on her lap went as white as if the colour had been literally wiped away from her face, and Elizabeth, fumbling with her seat belt, noticed immediately that she made no attempt to comply with the pilot's request and secure the leather strap in front of her. Elizabeth leant across to her and offered to hold the baby while she took the necessary precautions, but the mother merely clutched the child and stared stonily out of the window as the plane went into a kind of dizzy spiral dive and the rest of the passengers automatically closed their eyes and waited for the final crash.

The only thought that tore through Elizabeth's mind as they rushed earthwards was that the jungle, even if they survived the crash, would be scarcely more pleasant, particularly if it was the kind of impenetrable jungle that was still to be found in parts of Africa. And then, while she waited for the moment of disintegration, followed, she hoped, by oblivion, the pilot, as the result of a superhuman effort, managed to straighten out the machine, and instead of nose-diving into the midst of the gigantic trees that were now rising up on all sides of them, they did a kind of wild skim across the tops of the trees and landed, with scarcely more than a rather violent bump, in the middle of a clearing.

When Elizabeth opened her eyes it was to discover that the young woman on the other side of the aisle had fainted while still clutching her baby, and the baby itself was shrieking at the top of its lungs and filling the confined space with its cries. The two men passengers were slowly recovering their normal healthy tan, and the pilot was looking round at them and beaming triumphantly.

He had indeed saved them from a very unpleasant termination to their individual careers, Elizabeth realised, and she also realised that, now that it was all over, she was shaking.

But that did not prevent her from unfastening her safety-belt and going to the assistance of the young woman and the baby.

Later, they all stretched themselves out in various attitudes on the baked earth of the clearing, making use of any rugs or coats contained in the personal baggage of each of them, not only to soften the hardness of the earth, but also as coverings when the night swept down and the warmth of the day gave place to a rising ground chill.

Elizabeth sat with her arms wrapped about her drawn-up knees while the younger woman, whose baby was now peacefully asleep, unfolded to her the tale of her various tribulations and the unfortunate circumstances which were necessitating a journey to England. And although she listened attentively enough, and was full of sympathy for the unfortunate young woman whose greatest concern was that she had to leave her husband, and would not see him again for several months, Elizabeth, while she watched the stars prick their way through the dusky void above her head, thought desolately of her own future prospects – if, indeed, the future had any sort of prospect or hope for her at all!

At the moment she was surrounded by the jungle, and the pilot, after ordering them hurriedly out of the plane in those first few anxious minutes after the crash, when the danger of fire was the biggest danger that threatened any of them, had informed them all that there was no hope of continuing the flight, although it would almost certainly be only a very short while before other planes were out looking for them. In the meantime the two men passengers lent him a hand to build a fire as a precautionary measure against wild animals, and as the temperature was never likely to descend very low they were not likely to suffer any severe privations.

The baby had milk, and the pilot himself had produced chocolate and packets of dried raisins, and somebody had a thermos flask. They could hold out until the morning fairly comfortably, but after that it might not be quite so pleasant, especially in the heat of the day.

But Elizabeth was not really concerned with the physical discomforts resulting from the tiny aeroplane's unfortunate defection. She could have brushed those aside and dismissed them altogether if something more calculated to cast down her spirits had not been sitting at her elbow and reminding her constantly that she had done a foolish thing.

Not merely a foolish thing – a heedless, inconsequent, immature, unforgivable thing! She had run away from Nigel, although he had never done anything at all to deceive her, because she had expected more out of marriage than she was entitled to receive. Because for one thing she was so much in love with her husband that she couldn't bear, having married him, even to hear that his name had once been linked with that of another woman, and she had taken the jolt so badly that jealousy, when it lifted up its head, had made her behave like the irresponsible young woman he had once believed her to be!

She winced mentally as she wondered what he was thinking about her now, and what her father would have thought of her if he had been alive.

And what was it George had said about a woman measuring up to his high standards …? Elizabeth was quite certain that there was nothing about her that could measure up to anyone's high standards. But the question would keep recurring to her – Why, *why* had Nigel married her? There were so many other women, much more attractive than herself, whom he could have married … And yet he had waited until he was thirty-five to pick upon her!

Why …?

And George had also said that Carol Wainwright could never have meant anything seriously to him. Was that true, she wondered? *Could* it be true …?

In any case, it didn't matter very much now whether it was true or not, because if he really believed that a woman who incurred the responsibilities of matrimony should and must have "high standards", then hers had fallen so low that they could never be lifted up again! Not in his eyes, anyway. They were in the dust, and all her future hopes and happiness were in the dust, as well.

And it was no more than she deserved …

As the darkness deepened and the shadows of the jungle crowded in upon her she felt as if it was a darkness that was taking possession of her mind and her heart, and the shadows were omens of what lay ahead.

# Chapter Eighteen

It was about noon next day that a plane circling overhead located their position, and within another hour the unpleasantness of their plight was as good as ended. Another tiny aircraft made a perfect landing in the middle of the clearing, coming to a standstill almost alongside the body of the damaged machine. The pilot clambered out and waved them a cheery greeting, and everybody heaved a vast sigh of relief because the slow torture of the long-drawn-out and fiercely hot hours was over, and escape from the jungle was now assured.

Elizabeth was not one of the first to rise from her cramped position in the shelter of the nearest fringe of trees when the plane came circling in, because for one thing she was nursing young Mrs. Barrington's baby, while the mother enjoyed a brief respite. And as the others pressed forward between her and the aircraft when it landed she did not even see the pilot leave his cockpit. She was only aware that the tension that had held the people with whom she had passed so many hours – unforgettable hours while the darkness remained with them, and there was always the menace of something creeping upon them from the undergrowth – had suddenly lifted, and they were chatting and laughing and exchanging light-hearted quips, completely forgetful of their parched throats and the longing for something to eat apart from chocolate and raisins.

And as she did not see the pilot emerge from the aircraft, she certainly did not see the one and only passenger he had brought with him, and she had no knowledge whatever of his approach in her direction until he reached her side and stood looking down at her from an infinitely superior height where she was talking softly to the Barrington baby, and watching its china-blue eyes as they gazed solemnly up into her face. And it was not until a voice said, "Well, Elizabeth?" that she looked up and suddenly neglected the baby.

"Well, Elizabeth?" Nigel Van Kane repeated, and she felt she wanted to shrink away into the clearing as his dark eyes gazed back into her own, the expression in them quite unreadable.

Mrs. Barrington came hurrying back to claim her baby. Elizabeth rose and with a purely mechanical gesture dusted the dark red earth from the skirt of her sadly crumpled linen suit, and then, with a gesture that was just as mechanical, wearily pushed a strand of her fair hair back out of her eyes.

"Nigel!" she said, and that was all. Her voice died in her throat, and she swallowed hard. Her lips quivered, and she found it impossible to prevent them doing so.

"It's all right," Nigel said quietly, putting a hand firmly behind her arm and holding it strongly. "You'll soon be out of this and back in Baroti, and then we'll have a good talk about all the things you want to talk about. I've been"—his own voice seemed suddenly not quite so steady—"terribly worried about you, Elizabeth! It was a ghastly night!"

"W—was it?" She gazed up at him with unbelieving eyes, dove-like grey eyes that were heavily underlined by purple smudges, and beneath her recently acquired coating of tan she was almost transparently pale. She looked as if she was just about all in.

"Yes. The worst night, I think, I've ever lived through in my life!"

There was a curious twist to his lips that hurt her in some poignant way, for it suggested to her mind that what he was telling her was no more than the truth, and even then he was making light of something that had really been a shattering experience. His own face was far paler than she had ever seen it before, and in his dark eyes, now that the guard on what lay behind them seemed to be slipping away altogether, there was a look that, when she first caught sight of it, did literally take her breath away for a moment, and then set all her pulses hammering wildly.

"I'm sorry," she whispered, her voice husky with penitence. "Oh, Nigel, I'm sorry!"

"It doesn't matter," he said. "What does matter is that you're safe, and therefore everything's all right!" He slid his arm behind her shoulders, and held her tightly against him. "Everything, Elizabeth!"

Elizabeth gazed up at him with eyes so revealing that no one could have misunderstood what they were trying to convey, and they were so misted over with relief and happiness that some of the moisture welled over her eyelids and formed little rivers running down her cheeks. Her husband removed his speckless handkerchief from his pocket and carefully wiped away the rivers.

"Everything?" Elizabeth breathed.

"Everything, my darling!" He drew her into the deeper shade of the trees, where the fierce heat of the sun could not penetrate, and the eyes of their fellow human beings could not follow them either. "The pilot has told me that he hasn't enough room for all your people and the chap who was handling the other plane as well, so he's going to make a return flight, which probably won't be for another hour or more. Do you think you could endure to stay here for that length of time with me, Elizabeth?"

He was looking at her anxiously in the gloom of the trees, but colour was palpitating like a nervous pulse in Elizabeth's cheeks, and she nodded her head without uttering a sound.

"You're sure?"

"Quite sure!"

"Because I can remain here alone, and you've had a pretty rotten time. I think you ought to be got back to civilisation without delay—"

But Elizabeth interrupted him almost fiercely.

"As if I'd *let* you stay here alone ...!"

Her voice choked on the words, and his eyes developed an infinite tenderness. He held wide his arms, and Elizabeth flung herself into them, and he held her so tightly that for a few moments she found it hard to breathe. Then his lips came down and found her own, and there was so much hunger in the kiss that it was compensation and more than compensation for every moment of unhappiness she had lived through during the night.

Later, when the others had departed, and only the damaged aircraft was left to bear them company, he spread a rug in the coolness of the trees, and they sat down to wait for the return of the tiny silver bird that would fly them back to Baroti.

Elizabeth's head was drawn down on to her husband's shoulder, and his arm supported her strongly, while his free hand stroked her hair. He studied the fairness of her cheek as it nestled beneath his chin, and there was a faintly whimsical note in his voice as he reminded her: "But you *did* run away from me, Elizabeth – and really, I ought to find it hard to forgive you!"

"But you don't?"

She tilted her face and looked up at him, and her eyes were soft with happiness. He shook his head.

"Curiously enough, I don't. But that doesn't mean I mightn't think up a suitable punishment for you! For if it hadn't been for George Baker—"

"George?" Her eyes were all at once confused, and a rich colour flooded her face. "What—what did he tell you?"

"He told me that my wife had run away and left me because she was so much in love with me that she couldn't endure to stay!"

"Oh! Oh, Nigel!" She buried her face in his shoulder, and when his fingers sought to force it up into the open again she resisted them determinedly.

"Is that true, Elizabeth?" His voice was very, very gentle.

Elizabeth quivered from head to foot, but suddenly she looked up at him again. "Yes; it is true."

"Oh, my darling, my adored Elizabeth!" He crushed her up so fiercely against him that she could feel the violence of his heartbeats, and his lips moved against her hair. "Sweetheart, it was because you were so young – because I was so much afraid of doing the wrong thing and losing you altogether that I wouldn't let myself make love to you before! That I wouldn't even tell you how much I loved you! I didn't even know whether you had the tiniest bit of liking for me, and if it was only very tiny – just something that was beginning – I couldn't risk causing it to shrivel up just when it was beginning to take root …! Oh, Elizabeth, don't you *see* …?"

Elizabeth saw so plainly now that she turned her lips up to him in blissful surrender, and against his lips she breathed the words that delighted him: "But I loved you from the beginning! I *adored* you …!"

He gazed down at her almost unbelievingly. "Elizabeth, you didn't …!"

"I did!"

His eyes smiled suddenly, with a hint of their old quizzical look, and a faint gleam of mischief besides.

"Even when I declined to take any notice of you on board the *Star of the South?*"

"Even then!"

"My poor pet!" He held her with possessive closeness, and then once more he put a finger beneath her chin and lifted it, gazing deep into her eyes. "You don't want to hear me say that I was never seriously in love with Carol Wainwright? It was just a phase – and it passed!"

She nodded silently, but her eyes were reassured. There was nothing more he had to reassure her about.

"There's only one woman in any man's lifetime whom he comes to want above everything else," he told her softly, rubbing one finger gently against her cheek, "and that one woman, sweetheart, in my own case, is you!"

# FURTHER TITLES BY IDA POLLOCK

## Bladon's Rock (*as* Pamela Kent)

Richard was besotted by Roxanne, yet when Valentine was only sixteen she had fallen head over heels in love with him during a long and for her delightful summer. Now, some years later, all three were once again at Bladon's Rock, although nothing appeared to have changed as Richard still seemed destined to end up with Roxanne. Gaston, however, was also there. He had once remarked that they were simply ships that passed in the night, and yet …

## The Man Who Came Back (*as* Pamela Kent)

Philip Drew is a mystery. He supposedly arrived in the village and settled only temporarily so as to help out the local doctor. However, a portrait in Falaise, the manor house, appeared to be an exact likeness. Just who is he, what is he doing in the village, and what connection does he have with Falaise?

## Island in The Dawn (*as* Averil Ives)

Cassandra Wood made it clear to Felicity that Paul Halloran was destined for her. It seemed that Felicity was destined to live on a small Caribbean island in close proximity to a man she could never have as her own. Deciding that the situation could not be sustained, she driven to take desperate measures which appeared to fail and just increased he unhappiness, but then came a truly awesome revelation that changed everything.

# FURTHER TITLES BY IDA POLLOCK

## Flight To the Stars (*as* Pamela Kent)

Melanie was a junior when Rick Vandraaton found his secretary could not make a trip to New York and so asked her to accompany him instead. It was not long, however, before she regarded Rick as something more than just an employer. Her feelings only deepened when it became clear that Diane Fairchild had already ensured Rick was firmly in her grasp. Certain that Diane's interest really lay with Rick's money she decided to act, but what on earth could she do about it?

## Desert Gold (*as* Pamela Kent)

Martin Dahl made his dislike of Judith plain from their first meeting. However, he was the one person who could help her with an assignment for her magazine. She was writing an article about the ruined city of Bou Kairouan in Morocco. Eventually persuading him to accompany her to the ruins, she did not realise that in doing so she brought down the wrath of Natasha Frobisher upon her, who was obviously very interested in Dahl. He warned Judith that Natasha would make a better friend than an enemy …

## City of Palms (*as* Pamela Kent)

Susan noticed him on the plane bound for Baghdad. Indeed, every woman would. Handsome, almost magnetic in manner, yet somehow aloof and disdainful of others around him, especially inexperienced travellers such as herself. Yet when an emergency arose he was there looking after her and somewhat surprised then discovered he was in fact her new employer at the house in the Zor Oasis, her final destination. There, he once again came to her rescue. She had become embroiled in a frightening situation, the victim of a totally unscrupulous and jealous woman. Just where would this lead ….?

Printed in Great Britain
by Amazon